Happy 25th birthday, Harlequin Presents,

May the next 25 years be as much fun!

Love, as always,

Carole Mortimer

Dear Reader,

How nice to have the opportunity for a personal word. For we are kindred spirits, you and I. We both like to lose ourselves in the unique world of romance fiction. Where else can we be sure of "happily ever after," despite the seemingly insurmountable problems our hero and heroine are confronted with? Yet we do so enjoy their struggles, their conflicts and especially their passion. Passion for life, and for each other. Harlequin Presents® has been giving its readers passionate love stories for the past twenty-five years. If this is your first venture into a Harlequin Presents® or a Miranda Lee romance, then let me welcome you to our world—a world of excitement and intrigue, of sensuality and surprises; a world of sheer unadulterated pleasure!

Best wishes and happy reading during Harlequin Presents®' silver anniversary year!

Miranda Lee

Miranda Lee

MIRANDA LEE

Rendezvous with Revenge

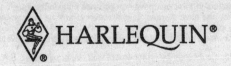

HARLEQUIN®

TORONTO · NEW YORK · LONDON
AMSTERDAM · PARIS · SYDNEY · HAMBURG
STOCKHOLM · ATHENS · TOKYO · MILAN · MADRID
PRAGUE · WARSAW · BUDAPEST · AUCKLAND

ISBN 0-373-11967-4

RENDEZVOUS WITH REVENGE

First North American Publication 1998.

Copyright © 1996 by Miranda Lee.

This edition published by arrangement with Harlequin Books S.A.

® and ™ are trademarks of the publisher. Trademarks indicated with ® are registered in the United States Patent and Trademark Office, the Canadian Trade Marks Office and in other countries.

Printed in U.S.A.

CHAPTER ONE

'WHAT do you mean, you're not going? Oh, Ethan, you promised! You've been working non-stop now for nearly two years without a holiday. If you don't take a break soon, you'll crack up!'

'And you call going to this type of medical conference having a break?' came the scathing reply. 'They inflict you with the most dreary lectures for the first half of each day, then expect you to come out of your boredom-induced coma and socialise for the second half.'

'Which is exactly what you need.'

'What? To be bored to death?'

'In a way. But I was thinking more of the socialising. What on earth is Evelyn going to say when you tell her?'

'Evelyn is the *reason* I'm not going.'

Abby grimaced from where she was sitting at the reception desk, trying to get on with her work and not listen to the private conversation which was unfortunately coming loud and clear from Doctor Grant's surgery.

If only Sylvia had closed the darned door properly, I wouldn't be in this embarrassing position, Abby thought disgruntledly.

'Explain yourself, Ethan,' came Sylvia's imperative demand.

'What's there to explain? I simply decided I didn't want to take Evelyn. Since this style of conference has been designed around couples, and I didn't want to stand out like a shag on a rock, I've decided not to go at all.'

5

'But *why* have you decided not to take Evelyn, for heaven's sake?'

'For reasons which I should have anticipated when I asked her in the first place. Evelyn's no different from any other woman I've been fool enough to become involved with over the past few years. After a couple of months they start fancying that our relationship—such as it is—should develop into something deeper.'

'Oh, how shocking of them!'

Abby winced at the caustic tone in Sylvia's voice. Not that Abby was on Dr Grant's side. Sylvia's brother was a cold devil at the best of times—something his older sister obviously knew only too well!

'Spare me the sarcasm, Sis,' he drawled. 'I never promised Evelyn anything more than the odd night here and there. She claimed that was all she wanted too, after her divorce came through last year, but she was lying. I should have known my requesting three whole days and nights of her company would be simultaneously equated with my feelings for her having miraculously blossomed into love, with a proposal of marriage imminent.'

'Silly girl,' Sylvia mocked drily. 'Though it might be fairer if you had a warning tattooed on that oh, so handsome forehead of yours, Ethan: ALLERGIC TO LOVE AND MARRIAGE!'

'Not allergic, Sylvia. Wary. As I am of all beautiful women like Evelyn. Most don't have love on their minds when they look to marriage, only money and position.'

Sylvia's sigh echoed through the quiet rooms. 'You still haven't gotten over her, have you?'

'Who?'

'You know very well who. Vanessa Whatsername.'

'I really do not wish to discuss the past, Sylvia. Neither do I wish to discuss my decision not to go to the conference. Now, if you don't mind, I still have a few letters to dictate here for Miss Richmond to type up before she leaves.'

Abby's eyebrows rose in a sardonic arch. Six months she'd worked for Ethan Grant and he still called her 'Miss Richmond'. Not that she really cared. It suited her fine to keep the disgustingly handsome orthopaedic surgeon at a safe distance. Romance was not on her agenda this year.

Or any other year, came the added bitter thought. She'd had enough of romance to last her a lifetime!

Still, his cold indifference to her as a living, breathing human being did niggle a little occasionally. He'd never asked her one single question about herself during the last six months. Not one.

Abby smiled ruefully as she recalled their first meeting. He'd been sitting behind his desk with his head down when Sylvia had ushered her in for an introduction.

Apparently, he'd given his sister a free hand in hiring someone to take over from her on a Friday—Sylvia having decided that after years of slavery to Ethan as both his housekeeper and full-time receptionist she wanted Fridays off. Her dear brother's only instruction had been that she was to train her Friday replacement thoroughly so that there would be no hiccups in her absence.

Abby wasn't sure what she'd expected after having met Sylvia. Someone older, she supposed. And less...striking. Sylvia was around fifty, plump, pale and rather plain. So when Ethan Grant had lifted his darkly handsome head and set his startlingly blue eyes on her, she'd blinked her shock for a few seconds.

Her involuntary surprise at his unexpected good looks, plus his age—late thirties at the most—had not gone unnoticed, a scornful coldness sweeping over those arrogantly handsome features, setting their chiselled beauty into a forbidding concrete.

'How do you do, Miss Richmond,' he'd said with a frozen formality which had never changed, not once in six months.

Abby found his chilly aloofness almost amusing at times. What had he thought during those first moments of their meeting? That she'd been bowled over by his brooding sex appeal? Did he believe that she might be harbouring a hidden passion for him, and that if he gave her an inch she would take more than a mile?

God, it would take more than tall, dark and handsome to bewitch her these days. Her experience with Dillon had taught her well. Oh, yes, the dear doctor had made her silly female heart flutter for a split second, but that was all. She'd quickly learnt to control any further involuntary sexual responses when she looked at him; just as she'd quickly learnt what kind of man lay behind his smouldering good looks.

He was a machine, not a man. A cold-blooded, cold-hearted robot who worked eighteen-hour days, operating at not one or two, but *three* hospitals. He even operated on a Saturday occasionally, if his lists for that week were too long to be fitted in to his Monday, Wednesday and Friday morning operating schedules.

Abby sometimes wondered why his patients set such store by him. It had to be because of his skill, not his bedside manner. He had consultations every Friday afternoon while she was there, giving her plenty of opportunity to study his personality, and she'd never seen him so much as smile at a patient. He would come out of his rooms and call each successive one in with that same sphinx-like expression on his face.

They were just cases to him, Abby accepted finally, not people. She wouldn't mind betting that he had never become emotionally involved with a single person he'd operated on.

Obviously, he never became emotionally involved with *anyone*, from what she'd just heard.

'There's no use bullying me about it, Sylvia,' he was saying in a vaguely bored tone. 'I'm not going and that's final.'

'Then more fool you! Any other man would just find someone else to take.'

'Such as whom?'

'Oh, I don't know.' Sylvia was beginning to sound very irritable. 'You could hire yourself one of those escorts, I suppose.'

'Don't be ridiculous. One of my closest colleagues will be there with his wife. Do you honestly think I would show up with an amateur call-girl on my arm?'

'How would they ever know?'

'*I'd* know,' he bit out.

'Are you telling me you've finally developed scruples where women and sex are concerned? Frankly, I think it's a perfectly splendid idea, and perfectly suited to your requirements. For the right fee you'd get exactly what you want from a woman and no more,' Sylvia threw at him tartly. 'You certainly wouldn't have to worry about her having designs on you afterwards either. You'd know right from the start that she was only screwing you for your money!'

Abby's eyebrows shot up ceilingwards. Sylvia must really be mad to resort to such an unladylike expression. Still, it was rather good to hear Sylvia get the better of her pain of a brother for once. Clearly he was rendered speechless by her acid barbs, if the sudden silence was anything to go by.

'Aren't you going to say anything more, Ethan?' Sylvia demanded after a short while. 'Don't you dare just ignore me. I won't have it, do you hear?'

'And I won't have you telling me how to run my private life,' her brother returned in an ominously cold voice. 'Now, go home and leave me be. I have work to do.'

Abby knew that tone of voice. And clearly so did Sylvia, who emerged from the room looking defeated. Closing the door distractedly behind her, she began walking slowly across the empty waiting room with a genuinely troubled look on her face. She seemed totally unaware of Abby's presence behind the desk, so deep in thought was she.

Abby's clearing her throat brought her head up with a startled gasp. 'Oh, my goodness, Abby! I forgot you were still here.'

'Would you like a cup of tea, Sylvia?' Abby offered. 'You seem a little... upset.'

Sylvia sighed. 'No, thanks, but thanks for offering. You're a sweet girl. I'd better go home and get dinner started. It's time you went home too, isn't it? It's after five.'

'Dr Grant hasn't finished dictating today's letters. I'll have to stay back till I've typed them up. You know how particular he is about that.'

'What a slave-driver that man is! Make sure you put down the overtime.'

'Oh, I will; don't you worry.'

Sylvia gave her a sharp glance. 'Are you having money problems, Abby?'

'I'm always having money problems.' The money she earned from her one day here plus her weekend waitressing job was just enough to make ends meet, with nothing left over for emergencies or luxuries.

'No luck getting a permanent position yet?'

'Unfortunately no.' Despite spending every spare second and cent having her résumé photocopied and sending it off in answer to every suitable job advertisement. The local unemployment office was getting sick of the sight of her, as well.

'I don't understand that at all. I would have thought some big flashy company would have snapped up a good-looking girl like you for their front desk.'

Abby just shrugged. She didn't want to tell Sylvia the probable reason that her application was passed over most of the time. They obviously took one look at where she'd taken her secretarial course and immediately put her résumé aside.

Sylvia had never asked for a written or detailed application, naïvely hiring Abby on just a telephone call and one short personal interview, blindly believing her when she'd said she'd been overseas on a working holiday for a few years and had no recent employment history in Australia.

Abby had not liked lying to her—she'd taken to Sylvia straight away—but poverty did rather make one desperate. She took some comfort from the fact that the glowing personal reference she'd been able to supply had been the genuine article and not a forgery. Dear Miss Blanchford... Abby was so grateful to her.

'I *did* get one interview earlier this week,' she admitted, cringing inside as she recalled the smarmy manner of the man who'd interviewed her. No way would she take *that* job, even if it was offered to her.

'Oh? Who with?'

'A small car-repair company in Alexandria.'

Sylvia's nose wrinkled. 'Surely you could do better than that.'

'I was hoping to, but times are tough.'

'I'll ask Ethan to find out if any doctor he knows requires a full-time receptionist,' Sylvia said kindly. 'Not that I want you to go. I'm really going to miss you. Ethan will too. He just doesn't know what a gem we found in you. You're always so willing to work back. Most pretty young things would be out of here like a shot on a Friday night.'

'I'm not that young, Sylvia.'

'Which is another thing I don't understand—how you got to be twenty-five years old without some lucky man snapping you up as well.'

'I guess I'm just not the type men snap up,' Abby said, smiling wryly as she glanced up at Sylvia. Her smile faded when she found that Ethan had come out of his rooms and was standing in the middle of the waiting room watching her, a drily cynical amusement in his cold blue eyes.

You're right there, darling, they seemed to say. You're the type men take to bed, not to the altar.

Resentment at his ongoing and unjustified assessment of her character sent her nostrils flaring and her heart thudding angrily. Who in hell did he think he was, judging her like that, and on such superficial evidence?

Abby was well aware that she hadn't been behind the door when God gave out looks. But she'd never been a flaunter of her various feminine attributes, or a flirt. And she had only had one lover in her life!

Admittedly she'd dressed and acted a bit more provocatively during her months as Dillon's girlfriend—he'd liked her in tight tops and short skirts and skimpy bikinis, and she'd been too besotted to deny him anything. He hadn't minded other men looking at her either, had seemed to enjoy their wanting what he had.

But nowadays she played down her sex appeal, using no make-up and wearing her long honey-brown hair in a simple plait most of the time. She never highlighted her full mouth with lipstick and did her best to keep her smiles to a minimum after her sleazy landlord had told her that her cool grey eyes took on a 'come hither' sparkle whenever she smiled.

'Is there something I can do for you, Doctor?' she asked, congratulating herself on the coolly delivered question.

He arched a cooler eyebrow back at her. 'Just three letters to type, thank you, Miss Richmond. After that, you can go home.'

Sylvia made an exasperated sound. 'For goodness' sake, when are you two going to start calling each other by your first names?'

When hell freezes over, Abby thought tartly.

'Miss Richmond would not appreciate my being familiar with her—would you, Miss Richmond?'

Their eyes clashed and Abby saw the mockery in his. She decided that two could play that game. 'I think a certain decorum is called for during surgery hours. Of course, if Dr Grant wants me to call him Ethan after hours, then he only has to say so.' Her steely gaze was drily challenging, but it didn't faze the robot one bit.

'I think we'll keep the status quo for now,' he countered without turning a hair. 'Shouldn't you be off, Sylvia? It's getting late.'

Exasperation was written all over his sister. 'One day, Ethan,' she muttered as she stalked out, banging the door behind her.

Abby hoped that she'd be around to see this unlikely comeuppance. But she doubted it. Ethan Grant couldn't be emotionally hurt because he didn't *feel*.

Or did he?

Sylvia's earlier accusation that he was still getting over some woman named Vanessa popped back into Abby's head. She stared at him, wondering if that could explain his attitude towards her. Had he been jilted once by some pretty young woman? Was she still embittered years later?

Abby could appreciate how that might happen. She herself knew that it would be many years before she got over what Dillon had done to her. But she'd never attributed such sensitivity to the male sex, and especially not to a man like Ethan Grant, who didn't seem to have a sensitive bone in his body.

'Do I have a pimple on my nose, Miss Richmond?' Ethan Grant asked archly. 'You're staring at me.'

'Sorry, Doctor. I wasn't really staring at you. I was off in another world.'

'Not a pleasant one, by the look on your face.'

'No,' she agreed drily. Memories of Dillon and what he'd done never inspired her to do the Highland Fling.

'You're not the most communicative female, are you?' he said, a flash of irritation crossing his normally impassive face. 'Here. Make sure you post all the letters on your way home,' he said as he handed over the small tape recorder, then whirled to stride back into his room, his white coat flapping rather angrily around his legs.

Abby stared after him with rounded eyes, aware that she'd just seen Ethan Grant not quite his usual, coolly composed self.

What had disturbed his equilibrium? she puzzled. His earlier argument with Sylvia? Surely not his discovering that his latest ladyfriend wanted more of him than the occasional dinner date. He'd been coldly contemptuous about that.

No, it had been something to do with *her*. Probably her staring at him. He hadn't liked that one bit. He also hadn't liked her not revealing what lay behind her preoccupation.

Well, that's too bad, Abby thought caustically as she settled down behind her computer to begin typing up the letters.

She hadn't typed more than a heading when a bitter smile tugged at her mouth. God, she could just imagine Ethan Grant's reaction if she'd told him she was thinking about her bastard of an ex-boyfriend, and how *his* betrayal had sent her to prison for four years—four long, hard, soul-destroying years.

Abby didn't think that what had happened to the dear doctor via the hands of that Vanessa woman would match what Dillon had put her through. If anyone had the right to be bitter and wary about the opposite sex, it was Abigail Rose-Maree Richmond!

CHAPTER TWO

ABBY was just beginning the second letter when she remembered the *other* letter—the one she'd forgotten to give to Ethan.

All the mail had been delivered extra late that day, *after* Dr Grant had started seeing patients. Not that he ever opened the mail himself, unless it was marked 'Confidential' or 'Private'.

Such an occurrence was rare. Most letters sent to the surgery were either cheques for unpaid accounts, general enquiries from other doctors, or advertising mail from various pharmaceutical and medical companies. But there was one letter that Friday which Abby thought the doctor might want to see personally.

It was from the Bungarla private hotel where the medical conference was being held—a notice about a last-minute change of lecturer. It seemed that one of the Sydney surgeons listed to lecture was unavailable, and was being replaced by world-famous neurosurgeon Dr Philip Ballistrat.

Abby appreciated that Ethan probably wouldn't care less about it, now that he'd decided not to go, but since she wasn't supposed to know about that she thought she'd better take it in to him.

Sighing, she pressed pause on the tape recorder, picked up the envelope in question and rose to make her way across the waiting room floor. She stopped in front of the closed door, glancing down to check that all the buttons on her white blouse were safely done up before smoothing the pleated black skirt down over her hips.

Abby didn't want a repeat of the unfortunate incident a couple of weeks back when, unbeknownst to her, one of the small pearl buttons on her blouse had popped open, giving anyone who had looked at her chest at an angle an eyeful of lace-encased breasts.

'It seems one of your buttons has lost its battle against your womanly shape, Miss Richmond,' Ethan had pointed out in a softly mocking voice as he'd bent to pick up his next patient's file from the tray beside her. 'Perhaps larger buttons are called for in future? Or even a bigger sized blouse?'

Abby had been thankful that he'd turned away before her embarrassment had time to blossom into a full-blown blush. Which it had—her mortification increased by the way her breasts had immediately seemed to swell further, straining against her bra and her blouse, making her fumbling attempt to do up the tiny button all the more difficult.

It was the only time Ethan Grant had managed to get under her skin—sexually speaking—and she wasn't about to let it happen again. So Abby was disturbed to find that when she knocked on the door, her hand was shaking. There was also an instant gathering of butter-flies in the pit of her stomach.

Her scowl reflected her feelings. To have Ethan Grant reduce her to nervy state was irritating in the extreme.

'Do come in, Miss Richmond,' came the laconic invitation.

Gritting her teeth, Abby opened the door and went in, calmed by the knowledge that her private agitation was just that. Private. The man seated behind his desk would never guess from her calm demeanour and cool gaze that she was anything but totally indifferent, both to his personage and his looks.

'Yes, what is it?' he asked peremptorily on glancing up.

She stepped forward and deposited the envelope on the leather-topped desk. 'A letter for you, Doctor. It's from the people running the conference next week, letting you know about a last-minute change of lecturer. I thought you might like to have a look at it but I forgot to give it to you earlier. Sorry.'

He picked up the envelope and tossed it straight into the waste-paper basket in the corner. 'I've decided not to go to that,' he said brusquely.

The movement of light and shadow across his face showed dark rings of exhaustion under his beautiful blue eyes, and despite knowing that it was all self-inflicted Abby felt marginally sorry for him.

'What a pity,' she said, deciding to do her bit to get the damned fool to go. Love him or hate him, he was a good doctor and he really did need a break. 'They've been able to get Dr Philip Ballistrat in place of one of the lesser lights,' she said encouragingly. 'I would have thought you'd like to hear him talk. He's very famous, isn't he?'

Abby was taken aback by Ethan's response to her news. He remained frozen in his seat for several seconds, his normally phlegmatic blue eyes betraying...what? Surprise? Astonishment? Surely not shock! What was so shocking about what she'd just told him?

Abby was even more taken aback when any surprise was swiftly replaced by an icy smile which sent an oddly erotic shiver running down her spine.

'Well, well, well,' he drawled. 'Who would have believed that? You're quite right, Miss Richmond. I certainly wouldn't like to miss the opportunity of hearing such a renowned surgeon.'

He swivelled round in his black leather chair, slid over to the corner, lifted the envelope back out of the basket then slid back again. 'Thank you for bringing it to my attention. You've no idea how disappointed I would have been to have found out afterwards he'd been there and I'd missed him.'

'So you're going after all?' she asked hopefully, thinking how happy Sylvia would be.

'Wouldn't miss it for the world.'

Abby almost clapped her pleasure.

'That's some smile, Miss Richmond. I take it you won't mind my being absent next Friday?'

Was it his sardonic remark, or the intensity of his gaze on her mouth which rattled her? Whatever, her smile faded immediately, although her heart began pounding behind her ribs and she found herself staring back at *his* mouth and wondering how it would feel upon hers.

Abby could hardly believe her train of thought. Lord, she didn't even *like* the man. Yet here she was, fantasising about his making love to her.

Self-disgust made her stiffen inside. She straightened to her full five feet nine inches and delivered a cool look across the desk. 'It makes no difference to me, Dr Grant, whether you're here or not.'

His laugh was as cold as his eyes. 'No. I can see that. Which is just as well, I suppose. That way you'll be able to give the proposition I'm about to make a totally unbiased consideration.'

'P-proposition? What proposition?'

'Don't look so alarmed, Miss Richmond. I'm not about to ask you to do anything immoral or criminal. I am, however, in an awkward situation where this conference-cum-holiday is concerned. It's for couples, you see, and the ladyfriend I was going to take can't make it.'

Abby was taken aback by the smooth delivery of the lie. Funny. As much as she didn't like Ethan Grant, she'd never thought of him as a liar. It just showed that one should never underestimate the deviousness of the male sex.

'That was the main reason I'd decided not to go,' he continued coolly. 'Because it would be embarrassing and awkward to show up alone. Actually, my sweet sister suggested I hire a professional escort instead, but I'm sure you can appreciate that's not to my taste. However, it occurred to me just now that perhaps I could persuade *you* to accompany me.

'For a price, of course,' he added, before Abby could do more than blink her shock. 'I don't expect you to do it for nothing. Sylvia mentioned once that you work as a waitress on the weekend. I would naturally compensate you for any lost wages, with quite a bonus thrown in. So what do you say, Miss Richmond? Do you think you might be interested?'

What do I say?

Abby stared at him while she battled to control her simmering fury. I'd say not for all the tea in China, you presumptuous, patronising bastard. I'd say stick it in your ear. I'd say up yours. I wouldn't spend one hour alone with you, let alone three days and three nights!

'I'm sorry, I can't,' was what she actually said, congratulating herself on her silkily smooth voice.

'The boyfriend would object, I take it?'

'No. I don't have a boyfriend,' she said.

'Surprising,' he drawled. 'Why, then?'

'I wasn't able to work last weekend because of a tummy bug. If I let my employer at the café down again this weekend I'll lose my job there, and I simply can't afford that.' She couldn't afford to lose *this* job either, which was why she was being so diplomatic. She'd have just loved to tell the dear doctor exactly what he could do with his proposition.

'How much do you earn in one weekend?'

'Why?'

He sighed. 'Just answer the question, please, Miss Richmond.'

'One hundred and twenty dollars, plus tips.'

'I see. How long would it take for you to get another similar job, if you lost that one?'

'What? Oh, I...I couldn't say exactly. Sometimes you can be lucky, but it could take weeks and weeks.'

'Three months tops, would you say?'

'Y-yes.' What was he getting at? Why didn't he just let the matter drop? She wasn't going to say yes, no matter how much he offered her.

He picked up a small calculator lying on his desk. 'Thirteen weeks times one-twenty equals one thousand, five hundred and sixty dollars,' he calculated aloud. 'I would assume a girl like you would get plenty of tips, so I'll up it to two thousand dollars—up front and in advance. What do you say to that, Abby? Not bad pay for three days' work. More than enough to make ends meet till you get another job.'

His use of her first name did not escape Abby, and it sealed his fate even more than his demeaning offer. 'I'm sorry, but I must refuse again, Dr Grant. I'm simply not a good enough actress for the part. I think Sylvia's right. I think you should hire yourself a professional.'

'But I don't want a professional, Abby,' he returned coolly. 'I want you.'

She just stared at him, her mouth going dry. My God, if she didn't know him better, she might think that he really meant that.

'Maybe I should clarify that last statement,' he went on drily, a single eyebrow lifting at her obvious surprise. 'The reason I said I wanted you specifically is because I know that underneath your oh, so cool politeness you can't stand a bar of me. I have no wish to have to fire you afterwards because you've stupidly fallen in love with me. On top of that, I would imagine that in the right clothes you could be quite lovely. Yes...' His eyes drifted down from her face to the swell of her breasts. '*Quite* lovely.'

Abby didn't know which part of his speech infuriated her the most. Certainly the condescending and lukewarm '*quite* lovely' kept going round and round in her head. My God, if she set her mind to it, she could knock this supercilious devil's eyes out!

'Aren't you afraid my underlying dislike might show through?' she asked through gritted teeth.

'No. I have great faith in the acting ability of women. Besides, I never take out females who fawn all over me. Of course, under the circumstances, I will only expect you to pretend to be a friend, not my live-in lover. Consequently I will change the booking to twin rooms.'

Abby only just managed to hide her contempt. So Evelyn had been expected to sleep with him during this little jaunt, play the part of his wife without ever expecting to get the part for real.

Charming.

For all Dillon's subsequent betrayal, he'd at least been prepared to pull out all the stops in winning her heart before expecting her to become his lover. Nothing had been too much trouble—flowers, chocolates, candlelit dinners. He'd swept her off to bed with sweet words ringing in her ears and promises of forever. Whereas Ethan Grant promised his women nothing...except a cold-blooded, machine-like performance between the sheets.

Why, then, did Abby find herself suddenly wanting to experience that machine-like performance? Why, for pity's sake? It went against everything she'd ever believed about herself.

Heat rushed into her cheeks at the appalling thoughts which sprang into her mind.

'I'm sorry,' she said, flustered now. 'It...it's quite out of the question. I simply can't.'

'There's no such word as can't,' he bit out. 'So what's the problem, then? I would have thought two thousand dollars would have smoothed over any antagonism you felt towards me. Believe it or not, I can be quite personable company when I want to be. Look, don't say no straight away. Think it over and give me a ring at home on Sunday night around eight. Sylvia will be out, so you needn't worry about any awkwardness there.'

Abby decided that it would be much easier to refuse for the second and last time over the telephone. It was hard to sound convincing when one was blushing and stammering. And when underneath one was insanely tempted to say yes. My God, she must be going mad!

'All right,' she agreed shakily.

When the beginnings of a smug smile pulled at her employer's disdainful mouth, Abby's heart immediately stopped its stupid fluttering. He believed she'd say yes, that the money he'd offered would override any qualms she might have.

Abby's heart hardened further as she recognised that he might even suspect that underneath her surface hostility she was sexually attracted to him. This last suspicion closed the door on the subject. Nothing on earth would ever make her say yes now. Nothing!

CHAPTER THREE

NOTHING, as it turned out, except fate, and an old lady's heartbreak.

The first nail in Abby's coffin came the next day, when she quit her waitressing job after the boss pawed at her bottom one time too many. Then, on that same Saturday night, some rotten thug broke in and burgled Miss Blanchford's room. The poor old thing was so distressed that Abby spent the whole of Sunday trying to comfort her.

'It'll be all right, Miss Blanchford,' Abby soothed, after the police had finally left at around four in the afternoon. They were sitting in Miss Blanchford's room, which was the biggest and best in the ancient old boarding house, its large window overlooking the rather ramshackle front garden. Unfortunately, it had been this same window which had given the thief easy entry into the downstairs room.

Miss Blanchford shook her head as two big tears trickled down her wrinkled cheeks. 'All gone,' she said with a strangled sob. 'Five years' savings. All gone.'

Abby bit her bottom lip to stop herself from crying as well. The poor old thing. But, oh...if only she'd put her money in the bank, instead of in a biscuit tin under her bed.

The police thought the thief was probably someone who'd once lived in the same boarding house and had learnt about Miss Blanchford's distrust of banks—not an uncommon thing with survivors of the great

Depression. Unfortunately, the police also thought there was little hope of finding the perpetrator and recovering the money, although they hadn't said as much to Miss Blanchford. Abby had insisted on that. The poor old love was upset enough as it was.

The real tragedy was that the money had been to buy an electric wheelchair. Miss Blanchford was suffering a degenerative muscular disease which was making it harder and harder for her to get around in her hand-propelled chair.

'What am I going to do, Abby?' the old lady cried. 'I don't want to go into one of those government nursing homes. But soon I won't be able to manage on my own. If I don't have my independence, I'd rather be dead.'

'Now you stop talking like that,' Abby reprimanded, but gently. 'The police'll get your money back for you; don't you worry.'

'No, they won't. It's gone. I'm a silly old fool for keeping it in that tin.'

'Now stop that. It won't help, crying over spilt milk. I have this gut feeling your money will show up. Give them a few days.' Abby had a gut feeling all right. Her stomach was already churning with the acceptance of what she was going to do to get Miss Blanchford that money.

'The man was coming to show me a chair next Wednesday. He said it was one of the best second-hand electric chairs he'd come across. And only three thousand dollars. New ones cost a lot more, you know.'

'Yes, I know,' Abby said, her thoughts whirling along with her stomach. If Ethan Grant was willing to pay two thousand for her company, might he pay more? Three thousand, perhaps? 'Up front and in advance', he'd promised. If he agreed to her counter-proposal, she'd be able to give Miss Blanchford the money before Wednesday.

Of course, she would tell her that the police had recovered the money. Her old ballet teacher was very proud and would never accept charity. On top of that, she might ask Abby some sticky questions about where the money had come from.

'Come now, Miss Blanchford,' Abby urged. 'Dry your tears. The woman who put me through my paces at the bar would not succumb to self-pity. Neither would she despair so quickly. Give the police a chance. And promise me you won't cancel that man coming on Wednesday.'

'All right, Abby.' The old lady found a watery smile from somewhere. 'Whatever would I do without you?'

'You'd do just fine, like always,' Abby reassured her old friend. Privately, however, she wasn't so sure. The once seemingly indestructible old lady was looking very frail today.

'I still can't get over my good fortune in your coming to live here. You're so good to me, Abby. Reading to me and playing cards with me. You're not going to move out after you get a full-time job, are you? I know this is not the nicest place in the world...'

Nice! It was a dump—the old house crumbling around them. But it was cheap, and only a short train ride from the city centre. She'd been given the address by a cellmate, and had hoped that she wouldn't need it. She'd hoped to be able to live at home.

But when she'd arrived at the house the day she'd been let out of prison six months earlier, there had been a message from her father saying that she was not welcome there, though he'd magnanimously said that she could take her personal belongings. She'd been so upset, however, that she'd left the house without taking anything, relying instead on the clothes she'd brought from prison.

The decrepit old boarding house had come as a bit of a shock to begin with, but not as much of a shock as the inhabitant of the downstairs front room.

Miss Blanchford had taught Abby ballet from the age of three till Abby had been shipped off to a private boarding school during her twelfth year. She hadn't seen her dance teacher since then, but had never forgotten her, having always admired her staunch sense of self-discipline. She probably had Miss Blanchford to thank for instilling in her enough strength of character to sustain her during her dark days in prison.

It seemed that Miss Blanchford had never forgotten Abby either, her face lighting up with pleasure once she recognised her old pupil. She and Abby had talked for ages, and Abby had told her everything that had happened to her in the intervening years. It had been wonderful to find a sympathetic ear and a shoulder to cry on.

Miss Blanchford's friendship meant the world to Abby, and she could not bear to see the old lady so unhappy. She vowed to do whatever was necessary to get her the money she needed for that wheelchair. She leant forward and patted the old lady's knees. They felt very thin and bony through the crocheted rug.

'Now, don't you go worrying,' she said softly. 'If I ever move then you'll come with me. And we're going to get you that wheelchair, come hell or high water!'

At eight that evening, Abby set about putting her mouth where her vows were. She walked down to the telephone booth on the corner and dialled Ethan Grant's home number. It killed her to lower her pride this way, but, given that there was no viable alternative, Abby resolved to do it with style—priority number one being that her lordly employer never twig onto her unfortunate weakness in finding him attractive.

'Ethan Grant speaking,' he answered coolly, and another of those erotic shivers rippled down Abby's spine. Damn, but he did have an incredibly sensual voice, once one was attuned to it.

'Abigail Richmond here, Dr Grant,' she said as soon as she'd gathered herself.

'Ah yes, Miss Richmond. I've been expecting your call.'

Abby hoped that her counter-proposal would wipe some of the smugness out of that sexy damned voice.

'I've thought about your offer, Dr Grant,' she said in a marvellously matter-of-fact tone, 'and I've decided I should be able to accommodate you . . .' She paused just long enough for his male ego to swell further before adding, 'For a price, that is.'

His sharply indrawn breath rasped down the line, followed by a few seconds of taut silence.

'I've already offered you two thousand dollars,' he resumed at last, not a trace of sexiness left in his voice. It was as cold as an arctic blizzard. 'I would have thought that more than sufficed for the job.'

'I'm sorry, but it doesn't.'

'I see,' he grated out, with a derisive edge added to the chilly reproach. 'How much would be enough, then?'

'Three thousand.'

'That's one thousand a day!'

'That's my price, Dr Grant. Take it or leave it.'

His laughter surprised then unnerved her. 'Oh, I'll take it, Miss Richmond, but only on one condition.'

'And what condition is that?'

'I don't have to change the room booking. Frankly, for reasons which I have no intention of explaining, I would prefer to pretend we were lovers, not just friends. Naturally I do not expect you to sleep in the same bed with me. I will make sure our room has a convertible sofa which will guarantee separate sleeping arrangements.'

'And if I say no?'

'Then you say no, and I'll make other arrangements.'

Abby only had to think of Miss Blanchford's despairing depression to know that she would never say no. But she detested Ethan Grant for manoeuvring her into a corner like this.

Still, there was no point in prolonging the agony. It would only add to her humiliation. Better to agree immediately, letting him think that she wasn't at all fazed by this change.

'All right,' she said with a superbly blithe offhandedness. 'I appreciate that for three thousand you can call the shots. But I want it all up front and in advance, as you promised.'

Once again, Ethan fell silent on the other end.

Had she surprised him? *Shocked* him, even?

Too bad. This was business—the business of healing an old lady's heart and giving her back a reason to live. She had no sympathy for Ethan Grant's feelings. Any man who offered money for a woman's company got what he deserved. Which was nothing.

'I'll send you the money by courier tomorrow,' he said in a faintly sneering tone. Clearly she hadn't surprised him at all, Abby realised. She'd acted exactly as he expected women of her ilk to act—like a mercenary-minded bitch!

'Cash, please,' she snapped, goaded into speaking sharply by a fierce inner fury. Couldn't he see that *he* was the more contemptuous person, for offering her money in the first place?

'Naturally.'

Abby scooped in then let out a shuddering sigh. It was done and couldn't be undone. God, but she wished that she didn't feel so low. Anyone would think that she'd just hired herself out body and soul for life, instead of just her companionship for three miserable days.

'I suppose we should get down to details while we've got the opportunity,' he said abruptly. 'I don't want Sylvia to know anything. This is just between you and me. As far as my sister is concerned, I'll be going to this conference on my own. You must give me your word on that, Abby.'

Abby was thrown for a moment by this second use of her first name. Till she accepted that he could hardly keep calling her Miss Richmond. She wasn't about to argue about Sylvia not knowing either. Really, the whole situation was a tad tawdry.

And slightly mystifying.

She wondered why Ethan was so keen to have his colleagues believe his companion was his lover. Did he have a reputation as a stud to uphold? Or did he have some other secret reason for such a pretence?

Something—some feminine instinct—rang a warning bell at the back of her mind. There was more to this than met the eye...

But Abby could not allow herself to be swayed by worries and qualms of such an indefinite nature. Three thousand dollars beckoned. Three thousand very real, very vital dollars. Ethan's motivation for such a sham was his business. All she had to do was collect the money then play the appropriate part.

Maybe what she was really worrying about was how difficult playing that part might be. She hoped she wouldn't make a fool of herself and betray her own secret. Despite not liking Ethan Grant one little iota on a personality basis, she could not think about him any more without thinking of making love with him.

CHAPTER FOUR

'First things first,' Ethan continued abruptly. 'Your clothes.'

'My clothes?' she repeated blankly, her mind still back on her perturbing weakness for the man.

'You do own something other than that black skirt and white blouse you wear every Friday, don't you?'

Abby thought of all the designer clothes hanging up in her wardrobe at home in Killara. They wouldn't really have dated, being timeless classical styles. She didn't doubt they would still be there either. She would have no trouble getting them if she went during the day, when her father was at the office.

'Actually, I have quite an extensive wardrobe,' she replied coolly, resenting both the criticism and scepticism built into his question.

'Yes, but what type of clothes?' he countered derisively. 'You must appreciate any lady friend of mine will be expected to be well dressed. Nothing cheap or flashy.'

'I am *never* cheap or flashy.'

'You're certainly not cheap, I'll give you that,' he muttered drily. 'And other than one wayward button, you haven't been flashy either. So far,' he added cynically. 'But I wouldn't like any nasty little surprises once we get down to the hotel. Which reminds me—there's nothing in your past or present which would preclude you taking this job, is there?'

One very good reason catapulted into Abby's mind and she gulped. Surely there wouldn't be anyone at this conference who knew about her trial or her sentence? It had not been in any of the papers. Her father hadn't been prepared to help her with a decent lawyer, but he *had* used his influence to suppress any publicity.

'Such as what?' she asked, guilt making her sharp.

'God only knows. You haven't graced the centrefold of any of the better known men's magazines, have you? Or any of the lesser ones, for that matter. I'm well aware that Sylvia hired you without checking into your background too extensively. I didn't come down in the last shower, Abby. When a girl's hard up for money and has a figure as good as yours, she might be talked into doing things not too savoury.'

Any guilt disappeared as Abby almost blew a gasket. Not too *savoury*! What in hell did he think she was doing now, going away with *him*? Lord, who did he think he was, looking down his nose at her when *he* was the one paying for her dubious companionship? As for her figure... She was fed up with him equating her lush curves with loose morals.

'I've never done a thing I'm ashamed of, Dr Grant,' she said with cold dignity. Till now, that is, she added silently. 'Believe me when I say I will do you proud as your...er...girlfriend. You won't have cause to complain.'

'Mmm. That's to be seen, isn't it? By the way, can you play tennis at all?'

'Yes, but I...'

'You don't have to be proficient,' he cut in dismissively. 'Adequate will do. I suppose it's too much to ask if you can play golf as well?'

His patronising tone made Abby seethe. She'd only been going to say that she didn't have a racket.

If I ever get him on a tennis-court or a golf-course . . . she vowed blackly. Thank you, Father, for all those holidays filled with never-ending lessons. You did do something for me after all.

'Actually, I do play golf. A little,' she added, not wanting to give the enemy advance warning.

'You've surprised me, Miss Richmond. I would have thought your talents lay elsewhere than on the sporting field.'

Abby decided to ignore that remark. He would keep. 'I wish you'd make up your mind what you're going to call me,' she said waspishly. 'One minute it's Abby, and then we're back to Miss Richmond.'

'You're quite right. But I don't feel altogether comfortable calling you Abby. Shall we compromise and make it Abigail?'

'Whatever you wish. You're the boss. Just so long as I know where I stand and what to expect. Speaking of what to expect, *I'm* not going to get any nasty little surprises when we get to the hotel, am I?'

The silence on the line was electric for a few seconds. Abby had no doubts now that Ethan had some hidden agenda at this conference, and it was beginning to niggle her.

'Meaning?' he asked coldly.

Meaning what are you up to, you conniving devil? she wanted to say. What is making you pay three thousand dollars to have me there as your pretend lover?

'Meaning you wouldn't be the first man I've come across who was a wolf in gentleman's clothing,' she tossed back instead. 'I don't want to have to fight you off every night.'

He laughed drily. 'How beautifully blunt you can be, Abigail. I rather admire it. Actually, I rather admire *you*.

You are a girl of rare spirit and a quite tantalisingly enig-matic character. On top of that, you've never resorted to the manipulative ploys an attractive female in your position might be tempted to use. But, no... you don't have to worry about fighting me off. Rape has never appealed to me, and seducing you is not part of my plan.'

'What plan?' Abby just *had* to say, not believing his back-handed compliments for one moment. He despised her for some reason, and had never bothered to hide that fact. Maybe he despised *all* females with a bust size over AA?

'That, my dear Abigail,' he drawled, 'is none of your business.'

And that, my dear Doctor, is an evasion.

But she didn't say it. It really wasn't a wise course of action to persist, not if she wanted that three thousand dollars.

'Fair enough, Doctor. You can keep your little secret.'

'Ethan.'

'What?'

'Call me Ethan.'

'Oh... oh, yes, I suppose I'll have to. I hope I'll remember.'

'Have a practice right now, then. Say yes, Ethan. No, Ethan. Three bags full, Ethan.'

'Don't be ridiculous.'

'*Say it,*' he bit out.

Abby quivered deep inside at his darkly forceful tone.

'Y-yes, Ethan,' she started hesitantly. Then, 'No, Ethan,' much more firmly, followed by, 'Three bags full, Ethan,' in a dry, challenging tone.

'See?' he scorned. 'You didn't have any trouble at all. Though perhaps you could practise putting a little more warmth into my name between now and Friday. Say it the way you just did in the presence of others and they'll think you want to kill me, not kiss me.'

Well, they'd be wrong, she thought ruefully. She wanted to do both. Kill him *and* kiss him. Damn, but she was actually enjoying sparring with him this way. It had a decidedly sexual edge to it. Abby was hotly aware that her pulse had started racing and that her cheeks were quite flushed with an unbidden excitement. Thank the Lord they were on the phone and he couldn't see her.

'I'll see what I can do,' she said, surprised by her cool tone. Heavens, she was a much better actress than she'd realised. Who knew? Maybe she might just be able to pull this fiasco off without getting her fingers burnt. If she started getting too hot and bothered over the sexy surgeon, she would simply remember Dillon. Thinking of that bastard always had a chilling effect. If that failed, she would concentrate on a simple survival. Now that she'd lost her weekend job, she needed her Friday job more than ever.

'Tell me the agenda for Friday,' she said in a businesslike tone. 'What do you want me to do?'

'We're supposed to arrive at Bungarla some time between three and five. I'm still operating on the Friday morning, and I do have a patient who's travelling down from the country to see me that day as well. I told her to meet me at my rooms at one.'

'Do you want me to come in as usual, then?'

'No. That's not necessary. Be at the surgery by one-thirty. I should be finished by then. I'm told the trip down to Bungarla shouldn't take any more than two hours.'

'What do you think I should wear for the trip down?'

'Something casual, but smart. It'll be pretty cool down that way of an evening in the autumn, so pop in a jacket as well. And don't forget to pack suitable clothes for tennis and golf. Oh, and throw in a swimsuit. According to the brochure they sent, there's a heated pool.'

'Yes, boss.'

'Don't be cheeky.'

She'd be more than cheeky if she went swimming wearing the bikini Dillon had picked out for her five years ago. Abby had gone up a size since then, especially in her bust. It must have been all that lovely fatty prison food. Or the free doughnuts and cappuccinos she'd been stuffing herself with every weekend at the café, so that she didn't have to spend so much money on food.

She would literally have to starve herself between now and Friday if she wanted her old clothes to fit her properly, but at least she'd already made a good start. She hadn't eaten a darned thing all day!

'Abigail?'

'Yes?'

'Oh, nothing. Is there anything else you want to ask?'

'Do you have my address to send the money to tomorrow?'

His sigh sounded irritable. 'I'm glad you've still got your priorities right. Yes, I have your address. You'll have the money, in cash, by three at the latest. Is that satisfactory?'

'Quite.'

'And I'll expect my money's worth in return.'

'You'll get what you paid for. And nothing more.'

'I'm glad to hear that, Abigail,' he drawled. 'Because that's exactly what I am paying for. Nothing more. No complications and no consequences. See you Friday. And don't be late!' he snapped, then hung up.

Abby glared down into the dead receiver, her heart thudding angrily. At least, she hoped that it was with anger. Friday seemed a long way off, but it would come round all too quickly, she feared.

It did, dawning cool and sunny, a beautiful autumn day. The week, which usually dragged when she spent it searching fruitlessly for a full-time job, had simply flown. Any spare minute had been taken up with alterations to her clothes. Hems had been taken up or down, and seams let out where possible.

'Tell me again the name of the place you're off to, dear?' Miss Blanchford asked as she watched Abby packing the freshly washed and pressed garments.

'Bungarla,' she replied, smiling as the old lady manoeuvred the chair closer with a small movement of the joy-stick-style steering. In just two short days she'd become a real expert, whizzing up and down the hallway and rarely bumping into anyone any more. Seeing her so happy made the sacrifice of the coming weekend worthwhile. 'It's a private hotel just outside of Bowral.'

'And what exactly is it you have to do there?'

Abby swallowed. 'Just secretarial work. Dr Grant wants me to take notes on all the lectures he'll be attending.' No way could she tell the old darling the truth. She would simply die, then demand that Abby give Ethan back the money and not go. Which would be a little difficult when it was already in the wheelchair company's bank account.

'And you need all these lovely clothes just for that?' came her frowning enquiry.

Abby tried not to look guilty. She laughed, and hoped that it didn't sound too false. 'No, of course not. There will be some socialising in the evenings. You wouldn't want me to look dowdy in front of all those high-flying doctors and their wives, would you?'

'You could never look dowdy, Abby.' Sharp grey eyes latched on to the heightened colour gathering in Abby's cheeks. 'This is all on the up and up, dear, isn't it? I mean . . . this boss of yours . . . he's not the type to expect you to be anything more than his secretary, is he?'

'Good heavens, no! Dr Grant's not like that at all.'

'I thought you told me he was very handsome. And quite young.'

'Well, yes, he is.'

'In that case he's like that, believe me, dear. I've been around long enough to know that all handsome young men are like that. Unless he's queer, of course. He's not queer, is he?'

'No,' Abby choked out. 'No, I'm sure he's not. But there's no need for you to worry. He doesn't fancy me at all. Certainly not in that way.' Which was just as well, given her unbidden excitement over the coming weekend.

'What makes you say that? Why wouldn't he fancy you? You're a very fanciable girl. And you're going to look stunning in that dress you have there.'

Abby stared down at the coffee-coloured lace gown that she was carefully folding into the case. 'I might not wear this one. It's a little tight.'

Actually, most of the clothes she'd collected from home last Monday had been a little tight to begin with. She'd been largely able to correct this problem by letting out seams, but that had been impossible with the lace dress—all the seams being overlocked, with not a centimetre left to spare. She was only bringing the dress because she thought she might fit into it by the last evening—if she swam up and down the pool Ethan had mentioned for a hundred or so laps every day. The colour

did look well on her, and it was a dress she'd always felt
good in.

Good?

Her conscience pricked and Abby had to admit that
that particular dress had never exactly made her feel
good. Sexy was closer to the mark. On the one occasion
she'd worn it for Dillon he hadn't been able to wait to
tear it off her at the end of the night.

She wondered what Ethan would say if and when he
saw her in that particular dress, with her hair done up,
full make-up on and her diamond and pearl choker
around her throat. Seducing her might not be part of
his original plan, but it might just come into his mind...if
she put it there.

'Abby...'

Abby started, then glanced up from her suitcase, aware
that her pulse was racing uncomfortably. What wicked
thoughts that man put into her mind! 'Yes?' she said a
little shakily.

'You're not in love with Dr Grant, are you?' Miss
Blanchford asked worriedly.

'Lord, no!' Maybe a little in lust, she conceded with
considerable understatement. But not in love. No way.
The very idea was appalling!

'Telephone for you, Abby!' someone called along the
hallway. 'Hop to it. Chap says he's only got a minute.'

Abby couldn't think who it could possibly be. No one
ever rang her here. She didn't think she'd ever given the
number to anyone. Her only friends since getting out of
prison were Miss Blanchford and the other boarders.

She was hurrying along to where the 'in only' telephone sat on a solid table near the front door when she
realised that she'd given Sylvia this number, which meant
that Ethan would know it as well.

Her stomach tightened as she picked up the receiver, and her hello was taut.

'Ethan here, Abigail. I'm in between operations, so can't spare long.'

'What is it? What's wrong?' Her heart was already sinking at the thought that he was calling the whole thing off. Abby found her dismay highly disturbing, because it wasn't the money she was worrying about all of a sudden but the thought that she would not, after all, get the opportunity to display herself for Ethan in that damned dress!

'Nothing's wrong,' he returned crisply. 'But I was concerned over how you were going to get into town carrying luggage. I know you usually take the train and walk the couple of blocks from Martin Place when coming to work.'

'How on earth do you know that?' she asked, taken back.

His laugh was droll. 'You've no idea the amount of useless information Sylvia relays to me about her precious Miss Richmond. I assume your cash fee arrived without any mishap last Monday?'

'What? Oh, yes, thank you.'

'Then use some of it to take a taxi.'

'But I can't!'

'What do you mean, you can't?' he demanded impatiently. 'Good God, don't tell me you've already spent it all? The whole three thousand?'

'Afraid so,' she admitted, her lips twitching. In a way it *was* funny, the false things he kept thinking about her. Now she was not only a mercenary gold-digger, but a wicked spendthrift as well.

He muttered something under his breath which turned her amusement to annoyance. She hadn't quite picked up the exact expression he'd used, but it hadn't sounded at all complimentary.

'I won't be late,' she snapped. 'I don't have that much luggage. Only one suitcase.'

'I told you I wanted you to be well dressed!'

'I *will* be well dressed. *Very.*'

'Courtesy of my three thousand dollars, I dare say,' he growled. 'Still, I shouldn't complain. You only get what you pay for in this world. I wanted a good-looking, well-groomed woman on my arm this weekend and they never come cheap. But I'm also paying for no hitches, so do me a favour and catch a taxi anyway. Do you have enough money for the fare if I faithfully promise to re-imburse every single cent when you get here?' he asked caustically.

'Yes.' Just.

'Then do that. See you no later than one-thirty.'

He hung up on her again, leaving Abby disturbed and frowning. All thoughts of coffee-coloured dresses and seduction had slipped from her mind, replaced by a re-newed curiosity over what this weekend was really all about. What on earth was Ethan up to that he didn't care how much he paid to get what he wanted?

Her resigned sigh reflected the reality of the situation. Ethan was not about to tell her, even if she asked him straight out. He was paying for *non*-involvement.

And isn't that what you want too? she asked herself. *Non*-involvement. This ridiculous one-sided sexual at-traction is best ignored, not fuelled by wearing sexy dresses and thinking sexy thoughts.

The coffee-coloured number, Abby decided sensibly, would stay safely behind.

But when she got back to her room, Miss Blanchford had finished packing for her, and the lace dress was already under several layers of clothes. With the old lady's intuitive grey eyes upon her, she was not about to wrench the offending garment from the depths of the case, though she staunchly vowed not to wear the darned thing. She didn't trust herself in it.

Just do what you've been paid to do, Abby, love, came the voice of reason as she snapped the case shut. Nothing more. Nothing less.

If she did that, and minded her own business, then the only real danger Abby could see was that she might say or do something which would lose her her one remaining job—which would be disastrous for her present depressing financial balance of fifty-five whole dollars in her bank account, plus approximately thirty dollars in her purse.

Well, you'll just have to make sure you don't say or do anything stupid, came her stern self-advice. Stay cool, calm and collected. Don't resort to too much sarcasm, however provoked. And don't, for pity's sake, start drooling over the man—even if he stands before you stark naked in all his masculine glory.

Abby's stomach clenched down hard at this last thought. Of course, she had no real idea how Ethan Grant would look naked. Maybe he was all pale and flabby underneath his clothes. Maybe his broad-shouldered, slim-hipped, flat-stomached shape was all an illusion, created by the superbly tailored suits he always wore.

And maybe pigs might fly, Abby decided ruefully. Ethan worked too damned hard to be flabby. As for being pale...the man had a naturally olive skin, his colouring as dark as a gypsy.

No, he would look gorgeous naked. Of that she was sure. Gorgeous and sexy and all man.

'Haven't you forgotten something?' Miss Blanchford asked Abby as she swung the tan leather suitcase off the bed.

'Have I? What?'

'This,' the old lady said, and produced from her lap the most beautiful perfume dispenser Abby had ever seen. It was made of rose cut glass, and had a pink satin puffer with a silver tassel hanging from it.

'Oh, Miss Blanchford!' Abby exclaimed, tears pricking her eyes as the old lady pressed it into her hand.

'It's full of Chanel No. 5. A man-friend gave it to me a couple of years back, but the exotic scent didn't seem to suit an old spinster like me. However, I think on you, my dear, it might just turn a few gentlemen's heads.'

Abby was both touched and tortured by the gift. For she knew that there was only one man's head she would want to turn this weekend. Yet his was the last one she could afford to!

CHAPTER FIVE

THE taxi driver let Abby off outside the tall building which housed Ethan's rooms, dumping her case on the pavement before speeding off into the heavy city traffic. The fare had come to twenty-two dollars, which left her precisely eight dollars and a few cents in her purse.

Abby sighed, then glanced at her watch. Only ten past one. Taking a deep, steadying breath, she picked up her suitcase and forged through the revolving glass doors into the foyer. Her stomach still began to churn as she made her way across the coolly tiled floor and over to the bank of lifts. She dropped the heavy suitcase, hitched her matching tan leather carry-all further up her shoulder, and pressed the 'up' button.

The doors opened immediately on an empty lift. Abby picked up her case and was about to step inside when something halted her.

It was a voice in her head.

Don't go, it said. Run!

Run? But how could she? She'd been paid—up front and in advance. Ethan knew her address. And she was almost broke. There was nowhere to run to.

The rather irrational fear subsided as Abby rode the lift up to the second floor. Really, what on earth was there to be afraid of, other than her own silly sexual feelings for the man?

It wasn't as though Ethan lusted after *her*. It was a one-way thing, and easily hidden. Lord, she'd hidden it for nearly six months, hadn't she? She would simply go on doing more of the same for the next few days.

Of course, she couldn't help being a bit nervous about the coming weekend away itself. It had been some years since Abby had mixed socially with the type of people who would be at this conference. Still, she *had* been well brought up, with all the advantages excessive wealth could provide, and she didn't think that she would embarrass herself or Ethan.

Her education had been excellent, with the right grammar, manners and etiquette being ground into her from the earliest days. Not even four years in prison had tarnished that style and elegance which seemed unconsciously to cling to girls of her background and upbringing, though she'd certainly learnt to stand up for herself, and to speak bluntly when necessary—not always in the most ladylike language.

She could well understand Ethan's ambivalence where her character was concerned. Most of the time she was the polished, refined creature her many nannies and teachers had created, but occasionally the tough survivor she'd had to become in prison would emerge, bringing out a feral cat-like creature, who could snap and snarl with the best of them.

Abby took some comfort from this new 'survivor' aspect of her personality. She could always rely upon it to protect her—emotionally as well as physically. It called a spade a spade and made her see things as they really were, shielding her from that other idealistic and romantic fool who had once resided within herself—the one who'd fallen madly and blindly in love with a handsome creep like Dillon; the one who'd always steadfastly believed that she had to be in love with a man to enjoy sex with him.

Abby the survivor now saw that sexual attraction need not have anything to do with love. It was an animal thing. Involuntary and primeval. An instinctive chemistry which just happened when one was confronted by an exceptionally attractive member of the opposite sex.

Scientists called it natural selection of the species. A female animal was always compelled to mate with the strongest and best looking male of her kind, so that the offspring would be the strongest and best looking too, giving them the best chance of survival.

Abby knew full well that what she felt for Ethan Grant had nothing to do with love and everything to do with natural selection of the species.

She emerged from the lift and walked slowly along the long corridor, reassured by her thoughts. She was still fifteen minutes early, so there was no need to hurry.

The door to Ethan's surgery was open, but the waiting room was empty. When Abby heard muffled sounds coming from Ethan's consultation room, she dropped her case and carry-all near the door and wandered over past the reception desk and into the small tearoom behind. She could do with a cuppa; her crash diet this week was beginning to take its toll.

Still, she'd certainly dropped a few pounds, and with those minor alterations most of her clothes of five years ago fitted her well enough.

There was one item, however, which still worried her— the treacherously brief black bikini lurking at the bottom of her luggage. Definitely not a garment to be worn in male company now that her bust had gone from a B-cup to a C, her bottom following accordingly. She wasn't fat, but she was definitely on the voluptuous side. She'd have bought herself a new one-piece costume if she'd been able to afford it.

Abby finished making herself the tea and sat down at the reception desk to drink it, her thoughts returning to what had happened when she'd gone home last Monday morning to collect her clothes.

Her father had not been there, of course. When was he ever at home? And the housekeeper had been new. It had taken Abby a while to convince her of who she was and that she'd come to get her clothes, which fortunately had still been in her room.

Not that she'd expected them to be gone. Her father had never bothered to throw away her mother's things when she'd left him, why would he throw away a mere daughter's? That would have been like admitting that he was affected in some way by their behaviour.

Abby had taken away two suitcases full, not wanting to stay long enough to sort through them. She'd also thrown in some of her better pieces of jewellery—both to wear this weekend, then perhaps to sell at some future date, if she ever needed to.

It had been a depressing morning. Just thinking about it depressed her.

Abby was sitting there, feeling quite down, when the door to Ethan's room opened and a woman carrying a small child emerged. Both were crying—the child irritably, the woman with soft, heart-rending sobs.

Moved by their distress, Abby was about to rise and offer to help when Ethan appeared by their side. He didn't notice Abby, his concentration all on the woman and child.

'Come now, little Chrissie,' he murmured, gently lifting the tiny girl into his arms. 'You're upsetting your mummy with those tears.' He kissed the chubby cheeks and jiggled her up and down. 'I'm sorry Doctor's fingers were so cold. Next time I'll warm them up on a heater.

How about that? And here's something for being such a big, brave girl.'

Abby watched, fascinated, as Ethan reached into the pocket of his white coat and produced a lollipop in bright, swirling pink colours.

'Here, let me help with this naughty wrapping,' he said, peeling off the cellophane and popping the sweet into Chrissie's waiting mouth. The child snuggled up to him, contentedly sucking, one arm tight around her doctor's neck.

The whole scene astounded Abby. Was this the same doctor she'd seen at work every Friday afternoon? This kind, gentle, compassionate person? Where was the brusque, autocratic manner, the coldly remote eyes? Truly, this was a genuine case of Dr Jekyll and Mr Hyde.

'Please don't be upset, Mrs Williams,' he was saying. 'The situation is far from serious at this early stage.'

'I know, Doctor, but I...I can't help it.'

Ethan put his free arm around the woman's still shaking shoulders. 'I know, I know,' he said softly. 'You're Chrissie's mother and you love her so.'

The woman lifted her face and Abby could see the intensity of emotion emanating from those red-rimmed eyes. A vice closed around her chest as she bore witness to the strength of this mother's love. She would move mountains for her daughter. Fight tigers. Ford flooded streams. She would never abandon her child. *Never*.

Abby tore her gaze away.

'Come back in six months' time,' she heard Ethan tell the woman. 'And we'll arrange a fresh set of X-rays for comparison.'

'I'll do that, Doctor. And don't worry, I won't forget those exercises you showed me. I won't miss a day.'

'I'm sure you won't, Mrs Williams.'

Abby's eyes were still dropped wretchedly to her half-empty teacup when dark-trousered legs materialised beside the desk.

'I didn't know you'd arrived,' Ethan said. 'I didn't see you there.'

Abby hoped the face she lifted to him had been wiped of all the pain she'd just felt. Perhaps not, since he frowned back down at her with what looked like compassion in his normally hard eyes.

'Are you all right?' he asked.

His unexpected concern caught at her still raw heart, and suddenly she felt like crying too. She stared up at him with wide eyes, wondering if he would put a comforting arm around *her* shoulders if she dissolved into tears. Would he take her in his arms like he had that child, let her nestle into the warm expanse of his chest?

Abby knew the answer even before she pulled herself together. Never in a million years.

'Just felt a little faint there for a moment,' she excused herself, though it wasn't far from the truth. She picked up the cup. 'I'll be fine after I get some sugar into me.'

By the time she rose, empty teacup in her hand, she was totally composed, and Ethan was right back to normal. 'Don't forget to take the taxi fare out of the petty cash tin,' he said curtly, and spun away from her, already in the throes of discarding his white coat as he strode across the waiting room floor and back into his surgery.

'Mr Hyde again, I see,' she muttered as she recovered her twenty-two dollars as ordered, then busied herself washing up the cup and saucer. She returned to Reception just as Ethan emerged from his room, looking more dis-

gustingly handsome than ever in a dark grey suit, white
shirt and blue tie—the exact blue of his eyes.

His gaze was coolly assessing as it flicked over her
own appearance. 'That outfit's a distinct improvement
on that hideous black skirt,' he said drily. 'And I like
your hair up that way. Very classy.'

'So glad you approve.' Abby knew full well that she
looked good in the camel-coloured mohair shift which
subtly outlined her hour-glass figure. Five years ago, with
Dillon, she'd always hitched the hem up to mid-thigh by
adding a gold chain belt. Today she had opted to let the
garment hang to its more sedate length just above the
knee, and the only gold gracing her body was a gold-
linked necklace to fill the boat neckline and matching
gold earrings in her ears.

The set had been a present for her nineteenth birthday,
sent to her by her long-absent mother from somewhere
in Europe. Most of Abby's jewellery was guilt presents
from her mother. They held no great sentiment for her
but at least they were the real thing. Real gold. Real
pearls. Real diamonds. Ethan would not be able to accuse
her of decking herself out in cheap or flashy jewellery.

'How on earth you manage to get all of your hair up
in that particular style, I have no idea,' he said, almost
scowling at her French roll. 'You haven't had it cut, have
you?'

Abby was taken aback by his suddenly accusing tone.
Why should he care if she'd had her hair cut?

'No,' she replied, struggling to remain calm. But stay
calm, she would. By hook or by crook. It was the only
way she would get through this long, long weekend. By
not allowing anything that Ethan said or did to disturb
her equilibrium. 'I've had plenty of practice at putting

my hair up.' When she had worked in the prison laundry putting up long hair had been essential.

'It's very long, isn't it?' Ethan commented, still frowning.

'Yes.'

'You ever wear it down?'

'Only to bed,' came her crisp reply. Abby was no fool. Men liked long hair on women, especially when worn down. It was considered sexy.

She hadn't grown it for that reason. She'd simply not cared enough to have her already shoulder-length mane cut while in prison, then hadn't had the money to have it properly cut when she came out. Actually, it was very cheap to maintain long.

'In that case, I should have the pleasure of seeing it,' Ethan drawled, before walking over to pick up her case. His glance, when he straightened, was as provocative as his remark. His eyes were narrow and assessing, as though he was picturing what she would look like in bed with her hair spread on the pillow.

His pillow.

Abby quickly counted to ten before deciding that she was probably imagining things. That old natural selection was at work again, making her feel things and think things which had no basis in reality, only in her over-heated imagination.

Calm, she ordered herself.

Calm refused to come.

'I'll take that,' she said sharply when he went to pick up the carry-all which contained her money, make-up and hair things.

'Be my guest. Are you ready to go? You don't want to visit the ladies' first?'

'That might be a good idea. Won't be a sec.'

Abby stared at herself in the mirror above the basin after she'd washed her hands. There was no calming the faint flush which ran across her high cheekbones, or the sparkle in her eyes. It was to be thanked that a casual observer would not see the way her heart was thudding heavily within her chest, though her breasts were rising and falling in a panting rhythm underneath the soft wool of her dress.

'You're excited, aren't you?' she accused her reflection out loud. 'Not nervous. Excited. That's where the danger lies, you fool, within your own silly self. Oh, be careful, Abby. Be very careful...'

Without thinking, she licked suddenly dry lips before she left the washroom, leaving them shiny and moist— and far, far more inviting than she realised.

CHAPTER SIX

'WHAT was wrong with that little girl?' Abby asked abruptly, in order to break the awkward silence which seemed to have developed.

They'd only been on their way a few minutes but it felt like an eternity to Abby. She was much too aware of Ethan, had been from the moment he'd taken her down to the darkened basement car park and personally handed her into the passenger seat of his BMW. She had quivered at his touch, her fears of blindly responding to this man well and truly founded.

Her question puzzled him for a moment. 'Oh, you mean Chrissie. She has a scoliosis of the spine. A curve...to the left. About seventeen degrees.'

'That sounds serious.'

'Maybe. Maybe not. She's only fourteen months old. Some correct themselves with exercise and time. Some, unfortunately, do not.'

'What sort of exercises?'

'Simple things, really. Always holding her the one way. Making sure she sleeps on the same side—in Chrissie's case, the left. Making sure her spine is always well supported. None of those soft-backed strollers. I've also recommended hanging her upside down by the ankles twice a day for as long as she can stand it. The parents could make a game of it.'

'What about a brace?'

Not yet. Maybe, if there's no improvement in six months, I might consider it. Children hate them so—especially little girls.'

'You were . . . very kind to her.'

'I have a soft spot for pretty little girls.'

'You were sweet to the mother too. And she wasn't at all little, or pretty.'

He slanted her a wry look. 'Not what you've come to expect from me, by the tone in your voice.'

'Well, I . . . um . . .'

'A surgeon can't afford to become emotionally involved with his patients. Not if he might have to operate on them. If he did, he might become nervous and make a mistake. I broke a professional rule today. I allowed that mother's distress to get to me. But I'm fairly sure I'll never have to operate on that little girl, so I should be safe.'

Safe from what, Ethan? Abby wondered. Safe from making a mistake, or safe from feeling anything that might turn you from a machine back into a man?

'I still couldn't do your job,' she murmured.

'It has its compensations.'

The lights ahead turned red and the dark blue BMW glided to a halt, its expensive engine purring quietly as it idled.

Like what? Abby mused. Working eighteen hours a day, six days a week? Not having enough time for any kind of relationship with the opposite sex except spasmodic and strictly sexual ones?

Or was he talking about money—enough to buy the latest model BMW without having to think twice?

The lights turned green and the powerful car surged forward.

'Nice car,' she remarked.

'It does the job.'

His indifferent tone surprised her. Men who didn't care about cars usually didn't care about money. Her father adored cars, the more flashy and expensive the better. Dillon had been just as keen.

'It's also leased,' Ethan added. 'I get a new one every two years. I'm not into cars all that much, but women seem to like being driven around in a decent model. Besides, Sylvia says I have a responsibility to my patients to drive a reliable vehicle, and not to be stranded in the middle of the harbour tunnel one day when I'm supposed to be in Theatre. Frankly, I think she's more concerned about my making it home for dinner on time. She gets really hot under the collar when I'm late.'

'She only has your best interests at heart,' Abby pointed out, cross with Ethan for not seeing how lucky he was to have such a caring and concerned sister.

His sigh was irritable. 'Yes, I know that, but she's like an old mother hen sometimes.'

'I think she's very nice. One of the nicest ladies I've ever met.'

He glanced sideways at her. 'Do you, now? She thinks the same about you. It's amazing how quickly you women make up your minds about each other without anything concrete to base your opinions on.'

'Liking a person is rather instinctive, don't you think?' Abby said archly.

He threw her a pensive glance. 'First impressions can be deceiving,' he muttered, then swung his attention back to the road. 'Traffic's heavy, as usual. Damn, but I hate driving in the city.'

Abby frowned. Had he been referring to her when he'd said that? Had he changed his mind about her character, now that he'd had a bit more to do with her? She didn't really like him thinking that she was a mercenary little piece, but it was safer that he did.

Abby decided it best to steer his opinion right back in that direction. 'While we've got the opportunity to talk, Ethan,' she said matter-of-factly, 'Perhaps you should fill me in on exactly how you expect me to act towards you over the next few days. You said you don't like women fawning all over you—which suits me fine— but we can't go around acting towards each other like we normally do. People will think it strange.'

'What do you mean, "Like we normally do"?'

'Oh, come on, Ethan, do be honest. We rub each other up the wrong way, have done since day one. The office fairly vibrates with our mutual antagonism every Friday afternoon.'

'It does, doesn't it?' he said, sounding drily amused.

'Lord knows why you asked me to come with you to this conference in the first place,' she went on. 'You must have been really desperate. And you know darned well *I* only agreed for the money.'

There! She'd really spelt it out for him, hopefully putting them back to the status quo and their original underlying hostility. He'd started being far too nice to her for her peace of mind. Heck, she already fancied the devil. The last thing she wanted was to like him as well.

'I certainly hope so,' he said drily. 'As to my being really desperate, I thought I explained my reasons for asking you quite clearly. Your basic...er...antagonism towards me is a plus. I'm tired of women wanting more of me than I'm prepared to give. You, my dear Abigail, have admitted you want nothing but my money. I find that surprisingly refreshing and relaxing. Frankly, I didn't realise till this moment how much I might enjoy hiring a woman as my companion. It does free one from all sorts of tensions and pressures. I might give some thought to doing it again some time.'

'Not with me, you won't,' she snapped.

'Really? Why not? You still like money, don't you? You certainly spent my three grand quickly enough.'

Abby took a deep, steadying breath, letting it out slowly. 'You're a cold-blooded bastard, do you know that?'

Another set of red lights brought them to a halt, and Abby found that her heart was racing a lot faster than the idling engine. She held her breath when Ethan turned to lock his chillingly amused eyes with hers, before letting them slide slowly down to her suddenly quivering mouth.

'Not always,' he drawled.

'Most of the time,' she retorted, struggling to stop her thoughts from turning sexual again. 'And you're a dreadful cynic about women.'

His chuckle was dark. 'Only some women, my dear Abigail. Not all of them. I reserve my so-called cynicism for the type of woman who uses the gifts God gave her in the ruthless pursuit of money and material gain.'

'I suppose you've included *me* in that category, just because I accepted your offer.'

'You didn't *accept* my offer, Abigail. You made me a very cold-blooded counter-offer—one which showed your true colours, wouldn't you agree?'

'No, I wouldn't agree. But I, like you, see no need to explain myself to you. You're my employer, not my husband or lover. I had reasons for asking for that specific amount of money—reasons which I'm not ashamed of.'

'Ah, let me guess. You have an invalid grandmother who desperately needs an operation which happens to cost exactly three thousand dollars.'

Abby knew that she should be outraged by his sarcasm. But for some weird reason she found it funny. Her laughter first surprised, then seemed to tickle his fancy, which was not what she'd intended.

'You are a wicked girl, Abigail Richmond,' he said, slanting her a rueful smile. 'I think I could get to like you.'

'You mean, if you didn't despise me so much.'

He laughed. 'You sound like you don't mind.'

'I don't. I'm counting on it.'

'Really? Why's that?'

'It makes me safe.'

'Safe? Oh, you mean from my jumping on you in the room tonight. Don't worry,' he said, a dark edge creeping back into his voice. 'Jumping on you will be the last thing on my mind once we get to Bungarla.'

Abby stared over at him. She'd been trying to forget about his ulterior motive for asking her to accompany him to this conference. Now her earlier doubts and qualms came back with a vengeance. What on earth was he up to?

'You...er...still haven't told me how you want me to act towards you when we get there,' she reminded him, hoping to fish out some other information at the same time. 'I mean...if you want your colleagues to think we're lovers, then a certain amount of public intimacy and affection will be called for, won't it? For one thing, what should I call you?'

'Ethan,' came his flat reply. 'I told you...no fawning. Look, just follow my lead in public, be your natural charming self, and try not to look revolted if I take your hand or put my arm around your waist.'

Revolted? Abby suspected that she might just tremble all over from a perverse pleasure.

'I doubt if I'll go so far as to kiss you,' he went on, 'but I'm sure, if I do, you can close your eyes and think of your three thousand dollars.'

'I'll do that,' she said with seeming nonchalance, whilst inside almost panicking. God, what a mess she'd got herself into!

'No more chit-chat for a while,' he ordered peremptorily. 'I need to concentrate on where we're going. I'm not all that familiar with these roads.'

Once again they drew up at some traffic lights, a perplexing intersection on the western outskirts of the city. Ethan finally negotiated the right road and soon they were on the expressway south. Within another hour they would be in Bowral. And then Bungarla.

Abby knew Bowral, a small country town a hundred kilometres or so south of Sydney. She'd travelled there once on a school excursion to see the tulip festival they held every spring. It was rather a quaint place, dotted with tall English trees, antiques shops and stately country homes—some of them very large, with equally large rambling gardens.

Bungarla had originally been one such home, according to the brochure which had been sent to Ethan and which Sylvia had left lying around on her desk. It showed a grand two-storeyed mansion set in the middle of a huge manicured lawn. The rectangular façade of the house might have been plain, except for a white-columned porch and a spectacular set of semi-circular steps.

The rest of the photos inside the brochure showed a well-cared-for, well-appointed private hotel with an elegant, old-fashioned decor which looked both charming and comfortable. A newer, U-shaped motel-style wing had been added behind the main house, and here the guests were accommodated in lavish style—the original home containing the conference rooms plus the dining rooms and general living areas.

The heated pool Ethan had spoken of was in a separate building near the tennis-courts. The eighteen-hole golf-course lay at the end of a short walk through the back garden.

Under other circumstances Abby would have been really looking forward to her stay there. The meals were sure to be marvellous and it would be wonderful to be pampered for a change. But she knew that it would not be easy to relax while pretending to be something she wasn't and worrying all the time about when Ethan might kiss her, or something equally hazardous. It was one thing to hide this unwanted attraction in the cool climate of the office, where they were employer and employee. Quite another in the strained atmosphere of a pretend relationship and a shared hotel room.

Abby scooped in a shaky breath, turning her head towards the passenger window as she slowly let it out. She would have to keep her wits about her if she meant to survive this situation totally unscathed. Either way, she could see that her Friday job might have to go. Come next week, she would double her efforts in finding a full-time job, thereby eventually removing Ethan Grant from her life.

Abby sighed at the involuntary feeling of loss this last thought evoked. It just showed how lonely her life had become if she was going to miss Ethan Grant. Or was it Sylvia she'd miss most? Sylvia with her no-nonsense ways and kind heart. Yes, that was more like it.

When Abby had first come out of prison and been literally thrown out on the streets she'd vowed to show her father—and the world—that she could make it on her own, that she was not the spoilt, selfish young rich bitch the judge and jury had believed her to be.

She had planned to secure herself a good secretarial job, find a nice little flat to live in, make some real friends who liked her for herself, and eventually marry some decent man who would give her the large family she'd always wanted. She'd hated being an only child.

But in the six months so far she hadn't even achieved that first goal. And her only friend outside work was an old lady she'd known from her childhood. The world was a much tougher and harder place than her privileged and cosseted upbringing had prepared her for.

But she wasn't about to give up. No way. She was going to make it, or die trying. Who knew? Maybe she *would* find a doctor who wanted a full-time receptionist down at this convention, as she'd told Miss Blanchford. There was no harm in doing a bit of canvassing on the side, was there?

At last they were whizzing past Campbelltown, the houses gradually diminishing on either side and the rolling hills looking browner and browner. Abby had heard about the crippling drought on the news, but this was the first time she'd seen the evidence of it for herself. She stared up into the bright blue sky and prayed silently for some rain.

Though on second thoughts, God, she added wryly, not for the next couple of days. I'd still like to get this patronising devil next to me out onto a golf-course or a tennis-court and whip his butt!

Shortly before three-thirty they made it to Bowral, the silence between them having stretched to close on an hour.

Abby might have been able to relax if Ethan hadn't grown increasingly tense with each mile. There was a stiff, strained attitude about his shoulders, and his eyes were fixed unwaveringly on the road ahead. Maybe he was always like that when he drove long distances, but Abby began to suspect that he was not looking forward to the conference with any real pleasure.

She tried not to be curious about this, but it was difficult. Try as she might, Abby could not discount the concern that she was a pawn in some plan which was not quite lily-white. Ethan had claimed that he was not asking her to do anything criminal or immoral, but what of himself? Was *he* going to do something criminal or immoral?

A shiver ran down Abby's spine. Curiosity killed the cat, don't forget, she warned herself, and steadfastly pushed the worrying thoughts to the back of her mind.

Once through Bowral, Ethan consulted his hand-drawn map then swung the BMW down a narrow, tree-lined road. 'The entrance to Bungarla is supposed to be down here on the left aways,' he muttered. 'Between two large oak trees. Keep an eye out for me, would you?'

'All right,' Abby said. 'There,' she pointed out ten seconds later. 'That must be it.'

In front of one of the huge trees was a discreet sign on an ornamental iron postbox which said simply 'BUNGARLA'.

The driveway was long, winding through extensive gardens and gradually rising to higher ground where the house stood in all its white grandeur. As they made their way slowly along the gravel road Abby realised that it was an even larger and more impressive place than the photos had led her to expect.

'I meant to ask you earlier, Ethan,' she said hurriedly before they arrived. 'Do you want to admit to my working for you?'

'Why not? It would explain how we met.'

'Yes, but you—'

'I'm not a snob, Abigail,' he broke in curtly. 'You can admit to waitressing too, if you like. I don't want you to feel you have to lie, other than about your relationship with me.'

'Actually, I'm not waitressing any more. I...er...lost my job there.'

He lanced her with a sharply frowning look. 'What happened? Did you ask for this weekend off?'

'No. The boss thought paying me my pathetic salary entitled him to further services.'

One of Ethan's eyebrows arched, his expression wry. 'One of the hazards of being so damned sexy-looking, I suppose. Did he fire you or did you quit?'

'Quit,' she said succinctly, a little rattled by Ethan's comment. Did he find her sexy?

'Mmm. I'd better be on my best behaviour, then,' he muttered as he slid the car to a halt at the base of the front steps. 'I don't want you quitting on me. Not during the next few days, that is.'

His sudden return to silence, plus his rigid staring straight ahead made Abby follow his narrow-eyed gaze. A black Jaguar was already parked in front of them, and a couple were alighting. A grey-haired paunchy man and a most elegant blonde woman. Startlingly blonde, in fact, her shortish hair fluffed out around her head.

When the man came round to take the woman's hand to guide her up the steps, she curled her arm through his instead, stroking his arm with her other hand as she did so. The man bestowed an indulgent smile down at her and began guiding her up the steps.

Abby snuck a sideways glance at Ethan as he continued to glare at the couple, his blue eyes ablaze, his hands gripping the steering wheel with grinding intensity. Was it hatred that burnt in his eyes? And, if so, for which one?

'Do you know those people?' she asked, forgetting her earlier resolve not to be curious. It was no use. She simply had to know what was going on.

Ethan took a deep breath, letting it out slowly as he uncurled his white-knuckled fingers from the steering wheel. 'Yes,' he admitted coldly. 'I do.'

'Oh? Who are they? Colleagues?'

'Not exactly. The man is Dr Phillip Ballistrat. The woman's his wife. His *second* wife. I'm surprised you didn't recognise them. They used to be in the papers quite a bit. Of course, that was ten years ago, when you were little more than a child.'

Abby frowned, a vague recollection of some scandal teasing her brain for a few seconds before bursting back into headlines in her memory.

'Oh, yes, I remember now!' she exclaimed. 'He was over here in Australia to do some operations, and while he was here he left his wife to take up with a blonde nurse young enough to be his daughter. The gossip rags had a field-day for ages. So he married her in the end, did he?'

'Naturally. You don't think home-wrecking bitches like that settle for less than a ring on their finger, do you?'

Abby felt the beginnings of a niggle about this woman, this blonde whom Ethan called a home-wrecking bitch with such vitriolic contempt. 'You knew her back then?' she asked nonchalantly.

'Actually, I did,' he returned just as nonchalantly, all emotion now wiped from his face and voice. 'She was a theatre nurse at the hospital where I did my residency.'

Abby wasn't fooled. The exquisite Mrs Ballistrat had to be *her*—the girl who'd once jilted him, that Vanessa person. Nothing else made any sense.

'Her name was Vanessa something or other, wasn't it?' she asked with feigned innocence, wanting to settle the matter in her mind once and for all.

'Yes,' Ethan admitted coldly.

'I thought as much,' Abby murmured.

So this was why Ethan had come. Out of a morbid curiosity. And this was why he'd brought *her*. As a salve to his ego. He wanted to see the woman he'd once loved, but under no circumstances would he want her to think he was still pining for her. So he'd hired Abby to parade on his arm as his current live-in lover. Male pride at its most destructive.

Exasperation towards the man sitting beside her swept through Abby. Why didn't he just let it go? Hell, she never wanted to see Dillon again, would not go one inch out of her way to cross his path a second time.

Perhaps because if I did see him again, Abby thought savagely, I might be tempted to kill the bastard!

Abby's eyes flew to Ethan's. Lord, he wouldn't do anything like that, would he? He hadn't come down here to exact some sort of violent revenge, had he?

The gentle and compassionate Dr Jekyll she'd seen in action this morning wouldn't have, Abby conceded. But what about Mr Hyde? The coldly embittered and heartless machine who also lived in Ethan's body, and who came out whenever exposed to the type of woman he had nothing but contempt for.

'I think we should get out,' Ethan said coolly. 'Henry's just pulled up behind us, and any minute now we're going to be descended upon.'

CHAPTER SEVEN

ABBY grabbed Ethan's sleeve before he could alight. 'Who's Henry?'

'A valued colleague, so be nice to him. But not too nice,' he added drily. 'My ladyfriends not only do not fawn over me, they do not fawn over other men.'

I'll bet they don't, Abby thought ruefully as she let Ethan go and waited for him to open her door. They wouldn't dare. Not that they'd be inclined to fawn over another man when with Ethan, she accepted. No other man would measure up. Physically, at least.

Abby wondered what exactly had happened between Ethan and Vanessa which had embittered Ethan so. She couldn't imagine any woman passing him over for the portly man she'd just seen. Even ten years ago, Dr Philip Ballistrat wouldn't have been any oil painting.

Of course, a nurse might have been very impressed by the famous neurosurgeon on more levels than the physical. Success was supposed to be a powerful aphrodisiac.

Abby suspected, however, that the doctor's appeal for Vanessa had lain more in the money which had come with his success. Ethan's contempt for mercenary women had to have some basis somewhere, and it seemed only logical to lay this firmly at the feet of a two-timing girl-friend with more ambition than loyalty.

Abby could think of nothing that this Vanessa could have done, however, that would inspire Ethan to a violent revenge ten years after the event. That kind of reaction to a jilting—or whatever had happened—came swiftly, not donkey's years later.

No. Ethan wasn't about to do murder. Not in Abby's considered opinion. It was probably more a matter of showing his old flame that he didn't give a damn about her or what she'd done to him. He was now successful in his own right, had plenty of money, friends and women.

Abby was still mulling over these conclusions when Ethan opened the passenger door. Distracted, she swung her long legs out onto the step without thinking, her dress riding up sufficiently to give Ethan a good view of her nicely shaped knees and slender thighs.

He looked too, one eyebrow arching at the sight. By the time Abby noticed what he was staring at, it was too late to do anything about it without losing her much valued composure.

'I almost have some pity for that other boss of yours, Abigail,' he said drily. 'You're a temptation, all right.'

Abby locked cool eyes with his mockingly admiring gaze before rising gracefully to her feet, her chin tipped back indignantly. 'Really?' She pushed the long, tight sleeves of her dress up to her elbows in an unconsciously defiant gesture. 'I find absolutely no pity for pawing creeps. How would you like it if a woman kept grabbing you on the *derrière*?'

His smile was wry. 'I suppose that depends on the woman.'

'Oh? What happened to your dislike of women fawning all over you?'

'Fawning in public and pawing in private are two entirely different things.'

'Well, don't worry, I won't be doing either!' she huffed, the hypocrisy behind her statement bringing a rush of heat to her cheeks. Damn, but she wished that he was as ugly as sin. Instead, even the most sardonic of smiles added a dazzling sex appeal to his already handsome face, the movement of his mouth bringing attention to the perfection of his flashing white teeth.

'Ethan, old man,' a loud, rollicking voice interrupted them. 'You made it after all.'

Abby welcomed the distraction, grateful when Ethan turned away from staring at her flushed face.

'I said I was coming, Henry,' he replied evenly.

Henry was a large, craggy-faced man, with a shock of thick, wavy white hair and a florid complexion. His wife, who was hovering at his shoulder, was a petite woman with bright dark eyes, short brown hair and a trim figure encased in cream trousers and a cream and brown striped top. She looked about fifteen years younger than her husband—thirty-five to his fiftyish, Abby guessed.

'I know,' Henry went on, 'but I wasn't convinced. I'm well acquainted with your tendency to opt out of these dos on the flimsiest excuse. I was sure you were going to say you couldn't find anyone to bring. *Again*.

'But you certainly have this time, haven't you?' he added, winking at Abby and ogling her figure with such uninhibited delight that she couldn't find it in her to be offended. 'So where have you been hiding this delicious creature, and when are you going to introduce me?'

'Henry, behave yourself,' his wife ordered from his side, though not with any great urgency or distress. Clearly she was used to her husband's flirtatious behaviour.

'Forgive my husband,' she directed at Abby. 'He can't help himself when confronted with a beautiful young woman. Thank the Lord he's a gastrologist and not a gynaecologist. Ethan, perhaps if you could do the honours with the introductions, we might be able to proceed inside. It's quite cool out here and my jacket's packed away.'

'Whatever you say, Ann. I'm easy,' Ethan said equably, giving Abby a glimpse of yet another side of his character which she'd previously been unacquainted with. A stunningly relaxed easy-going side. It seemed he had more personalities lurking inside him than just Dr Jekyll and Mr Hyde.

'Abigail, this lecher is Dr Henry Maclean,' he continued, in the same marvellously charming and casual manner, 'the most overrated stomach man in practice today. But a damned good golf player. And this is Ann, his long-suffering spouse and mother of his two equally long-suffering sons.'

'Three, Ethan,' Ann reprimanded, rolling her eyes at him. 'We had a third boy a couple of years back. You were one of the godparents.'

'Good Lord, was I? It must have slipped my mind. Sorry.'

'These slips of memory are a symptom of being a workaholic, Abigail,' Ann told her. 'There again, if you're dating Ethan, I dare say you already know he's chained to his operating table.'

'Only too well,' Abby answered, adopting a droll tone in keeping with the mood of the group. 'If I didn't work for him, I'd never see him.' And wasn't that the truth!

Ann's neatly shaped dark brows lifted skywards. 'You work for Ethan? What as, for heaven's sake? I know you can't be a nurse, or Henry would have already raved *ad nauseum*.'

'Actually, I'm Sylvia's stand-in receptionist on a Friday. But not for much longer, I hope. I'm looking for a full-time receptionist's job.'

'Good Lord, you mean that?' Henry exclaimed excitedly. 'You're hired! I'll fire my other girl on the spot the moment we get back to Sydney.'

'Over my dead body,' Ethan drawled. 'Abigail's going to work full-time for me.'

Abby turned rounded eyes upon him. He couldn't be serious. This had to be part of the pretence. But why, for heaven's sake?

'I've been thinking about sending Sylvia on a much deserved world cruise for ages,' he continued casually, 'and I think the right time has just arrived. So what do you say, Abigail? Do you think you could stand me on a five-day-a-week basis as well as at weekends?'

'Of course she could,' Ann snorted. 'Men ask such stupid questions sometimes, don't they?'

'All the time,' Abby agreed, in defiance of his springing this upon her. 'Ethan knows I'm his for the hiring,' she added with a bold glance. 'If the price is right.'

He seemed startled for a second, before a slow and very knowing smile pulled at his sensual mouth. Abby found herself staring at that mouth again and thinking all sorts of appalling things, only a porter's arrival saving her from another mortifying blush. She looked swiftly away, feeling totally irritated with herself. Talk about saying stupid things. She'd just opened her mouth and put her foot right in it.

'Let's go, Abby,' Ann said, and slid an arm through hers. 'The men can organise the luggage. You don't mind me calling you Abby, do you?'

'Not at all. I prefer it.'

'You know, Abby,' Ann said as she began leading her up the never-ending steps, 'I'm so pleased to see Ethan dating a nice young woman like yourself, and not one of those chilly pieces of porcelain he usually displays on his arm. Although I have to tell you I was surprised to find out you work for him. He's never even looked sideways at any of the nurses at the hospital. Or so Henry tells me, and he'd know.

'He doesn't miss a trick, that man. Henry says Ethan has this thing about not mixing business with pleasure. Not that Ethan leaves much time for pleasure anyway. As Henry says, it's a miracle he agreed to come here at all. But I suppose we have you to thank for that,' she finished, smiling over at her.

'I think you could safely say that's true,' Abby replied carefully while smiling back at Ann.

The woman was clearly a gossip, but not a malicious one. Abby rather liked her. She liked Henry too, despite his open leering. There was something sweet and endearing about both of them. They were also pleasantly down-to-earth, with not a trace of snobbery about them. Her estimation of Ethan's basic character went up a notch with his choice of friends.

'So how did you manage to get past that professional reserve of his?' Ann enquired.

Abby remembered what Ethan had said about being natural and sticking as close to the truth as possible. 'I don't know.' She shrugged nonchalantly. 'I certainly didn't try to. To be frank, when I first met Ethan I didn't like him one bit. I don't think he liked me much either.'

'Fiddlesticks! I'll bet he was instantly smitten but just didn't want to break his precious rule. So how long were you working for him before he asked you out?'

'Er... quite a few months.'

'How long have you been going out together? It can't have been very long. He brought some hideous Evelyn woman to a dinner party of ours a few weeks back.'

'Hideous in what way?' Abby countered, cleverly bypassing a direct answer to the other awkward question about how long they'd been dating.

'Oh, I don't mean hideous-looking. She was very beautiful in a coldly sophisticated fashion. But you could see that she kept sizing up Ethan like an antiques collector with a prized piece in her sights. I was terrified he was going to bring her down here this weekend. You've no idea how relieved and delighted I was to see you.'

Abby laughed. 'You'll be giving me a swelled head if you don't stop.'

'No, not you, Abby. I can see you're a girl with her feet on the ground and her heart in the right place. You like Ethan for himself, I'll bet, not his bank balance.'

Abby battled not to blush or look guilty as the men joined them on the top step, the wry expression in Ethan's cold blue eyes making it perfectly clear that he'd heard that last remark.

'Inside, my love,' Henry ordered cheerily as he reclaimed his wife's elbow.

'She wouldn't have said that if she knew the truth,' Ethan rasped in Abby's ear as he guided her along in the other couple's wake.

'Maybe Ann has more insight into the truth than you give her credit for,' Abby countered, stung by both Ethan's cynicism and the effect his touch was having on her. 'Not that *you* can talk,' she whispered. 'You lied just now about hiring me full-time. I'll bet you just didn't want me working for Henry.'

'Too true. But I wasn't lying. I do want you working for me full-time in the future. I have plans for you, Abigail, my love.'

'And you think I'll just fall in with them?'

'But of course you will,' he returned with silky smugness. 'If the price is right.'

Their turn to approach the busy reception desk put an end to their provocative sparring, by which time Abby's delicious defiance had begun to give way to a churning nervousness. Ethan *was* attracted to her, she realised as she stood there next to him. She could feel the heat beneath his bruising fingertips, had heard the ruthlessly sexual intent behind his declaration that he had plans for her.

Suddenly she knew what those plans were. He wanted her, not just as his receptionist, but as his lover. His bought and paid-for lover. His mistress, in other words.

Abby should have been outraged by the prospect of such an indecent proposal. Instead she was terrified of what her answer would be, if and when he made that proposal.

Ethan was given two sets of keys to their room and a uniformed porter carried their luggage ahead of them along a high-ceilinged wood-panelled corridor, through a sun-lit doorway, then along a covered garden walkway which led to the motel-style wing. A minute later they were alone in the spacious and quite luxuriously furnished suite. Abby glanced agitatedly around, her eyes landing on the bed to her immediate left.

It was king-sized and covered in a forest-green quilted bedspread, and a huge gilt-edged mirror hung with erotic placement over the darkly polished bedhead. Abby gulped, her nervous gaze searching for and finding what she hoped was a sofa-bed in the sitting area across the way. It looked too elegant to be a convertible, covered in a silky green and maroon striped material.

A large bowl of fruit sat on the coffee-table in front of it, along with a complimentary bottle of champagne and two fluted crystal glasses.

'Anyone would think we were here on our honeymoon,' Ethan commented drily as he walked over and picked up the bottle. 'At least it's a good brand.' He shoved it back in the ice-bucket and moved on to stare through the plushly curtained window, his face instantly becoming shuttered, as though he wasn't looking at the garden beyond at all.

'Why *are* we here, Ethan?' Abby asked abruptly.

He turned to face her, his far-away expression immediately replaced by his usual stony countenance and hard blue eyes. Mr Hyde was firmly in residence again.

'Pardon me if I repeat that that is none of your business,' he drawled. His tone was typical of the Ethan she'd come to dislike so intensely. Coldly arrogant and ruthlessly insensitive to her feelings.

When he behaved like this, Abby ached to give him a big kick. Since this reaction wasn't practical, she'd found over the last few months that acting with blithe indifference towards his black moods worked almost as well.

'Fair enough.' She shrugged. 'But if you want me to become your full-time receptionist I suggest you start treating me with a little more manners. I can bear your boorish behaviour one day a week, but I certainly could not stand it for five. And *no* amount of money would sway me on this.'

She lifted her nose in snooty defiance of his belief that he could corrupt her with cash. Little did he know that any corruption would have nothing to do with his bank balance but something far more basic, and totally free.

He glared back at her, the muscles flexing along his jaw, a furious glitter bringing a momentary fire to his normally cold gaze.

I've really got under his skin this time, she realised with some surprise. Good! I need to get this relationship right back to square one, which means bristling with mutual antagonism.

'I'll treat you exactly as you deserve to be treated,' he flung at her.

'In that case, I suggest you start smartening up your act, because I deserve a hell of a lot better than you've been dishing out.'

His visible shock was almost laughable, but *he* was the one who finally threw back his head and laughed. 'You have a hide as thick as an elephant, do you know that? Very well, I will play the gentleman with you, if that's what you wish.'

He strode over and took her hand, lifting it to his lips before she could object. She knew his kiss was mocking, but still it stirred her blood more than it had any right to. She stiffened under the surprising warmth of his lips, and he glanced up at her from underneath derisive dark brows.

'Not to your taste?' he taunted.

She said nothing, merely removed her hand from his before she burst into flames before his very eyes. Damn, but if this was what a kiss on the hand could do, imagine what would happen if he really kissed her!

Ethan shrugged. 'Well, you can't say I didn't try. So what were you and Ann talking about on the steps, before Henry and I joined you?' he asked abruptly. 'Don't hedge, now. I want the truth.'

Abby was happy with the change of subject, but not happy with Ethan's continued closeness. Whirling, she walked over and sat down on the side of the bed. 'Nothing of vital interest. Ann was saying how delighted she was to find you'd brought someone really sweet like me, instead of that hideous Evelyn person you took to their dinner party recently.' She batted her eyelashes at him and crossed her legs, swinging them idly to and fro.

Ethan stared, first at her legs, then at her face. 'So how do you do it, Abigail?' he asked, cold derision in his voice. 'How do you pull the wool over people's eyes so quickly and so completely? First Sylvia. Now Ann and Henry. Oh, yes, Henry as well. He virtually said the same thing while we were organising the luggage and cars.'

An indignant anger seethed deep inside Abby but she refused to surrender to it. 'Maybe I'm a conjurer,' she returned airily. 'Or a witch. Yes, that's it.' Her smile was one of wicked mischief. 'I'm a witch. I put spells on people when I want them to like me. Watch out, Ethan, or I might put a spell on you.' Dear heaven, but he did bring out the worst in her!

'There isn't a woman on earth who could make me like her against my will,' he sneered. 'My days of being blinded by beauty are well and truly over.'

'Then what were you doing with the beautiful Evelyn?'

'What do you *think* I was doing with her?'

It sent a chill through Abby that Ethan would ruthlessly take a woman he didn't care for to bed, simply because she had a beautiful body. Strange...only a couple of days ago she'd fantasised about his doing the same thing to her and had found the idea perversely exciting. She still found it exciting, but repulsive at the same time. How could one want something, yet be repelled by it?

'Yuk,' she said, and meant it.

'Watch out I don't put a spell on *you*, lovely Abigail,' he said darkly. 'I have a penchant for seducing beautiful women, and, believe me, I'm invariably successful when I put my mind to it.'

'Ah, but not with me, Ethan. My days of being blinded by beauty are well and truly over as well.'

'Are you complimenting me?' he drawled, unnerving her when his hands lifted to begin undoing his tie.

'No, I'm warning you not to waste your time.'

His eyes searched her face, noting, perhaps, its high colour and glittering eyes. 'I'm not so sure it *would* be a waste of time.'

'Touch me and I won't stay.'

'Do that and you'll lose your job. The only one you have left, I gather.'

Abby could only stare at him, truly shocked that he would stoop to such low tactics. And oddly disappointed. Yet she shouldn't have been. Hadn't she always known that he was an unfeeling and ruthless bastard?

Shock and disappointment quickly gave way to a blind outrage. 'God, but I despise you,' she spat, jumping to her feet and glaring her fury at him. 'Who do you think you are, threatening me like this? And who do you think you are, offering me money to come here with you, then thinking badly of me because I accepted? I'd actually *tell* you the real reason I made that counter-offer if I thought you'd believe me. But you won't. You like justifying your demeaning proposition by thinking I'm some kind of amateur whore.'

She was quivering with emotion as she stalked towards him. 'You can stick your pathetic job on Fridays. Plus your so-called *plans* for me. I'm sick and tired of you looking down your nose at me. Though why in hell should you? What have I ever done to make you think what you obviously think?'

She was close to him now. *Too* close. She could actually smell the tang of his expensive aftershave, see the sudden blaze in his eyes, feeling the heat of his own anger.

'I'm leaving,' she told him defiantly. 'And there isn't anything you can do about it.'

He glared at her, and for a split second she was sure he was going to grab her. Grab her and kiss her and seduce her, as he'd threatened a minute ago.

Her eyes widened as the seconds ticked away and she began willing him to do just that. Her head whirled as she struggled to gain control over her appalling thoughts and dangerously excited body.

What was it about this man that aroused such a primitive sexuality within her? Thinking of Dillon didn't help, for what she'd felt for Dillon had been nothing like this at all! There was nothing romantic or idealistic about her feelings for Ethan. It was just sex at its most basic. Raw and tempestuous, and totally without conscience.

Suddenly he spun away, striding across the room and picking up her suitcase. But instead of throwing it at her he tossed it onto the bed and snapped it open.

'Don't be so bloody melodramatic,' he ground out harshly. 'I've never thought of you as an amateur whore, and I don't give a damn why you asked me for that amount of money. I accept I was out of line just now, and I humbly apologise. Believe me when I say it won't happen again. Refuse my offer of a full-time job if you detest my company that much. Quit your Friday job as well. But you're not quitting *this* job. I've paid you to be my pretend lover for the duration of this conference, and my pretend lover you are going to be. Do I make myself clear?'

She nodded weakly as reality returned, all her pent-up emotion and tension abruptly draining out of her. Ethan was so right. Her own threat to leave *had* been melodramatic. And quite impractical. She didn't even have enough money with her to get back to Sydney on her own. No, she was locked in, and she had to see these three days through, no matter what.

'Now, I suggest you unpack and start getting ready for cocktails and dinner,' he ordered curtly. 'It's already after four, and if I know women, you'll need all of the next two hours to be totally satisfied with how you look.'

CHAPTER EIGHT

ETHAN was in the shower when the telephone rang. Abby turned from where she was putting the finishing touches to her hair, securing the sash of the complimentary cream bathrobe as she walked over to pick up the receiver from the bedside chest. Without thinking, she said the words she always said when answering Ethan's telephone.

'Dr Grant's room.'

Dead silence down the line.

'Dr Grant's room,' she repeated. 'Hello, is anyone there?'

'Abby?' came the startled query. 'That is you, isn't it?'

Abby's hand flew to her mouth. Dear God. Sylvia.

What to do? Hang up, or change her voice suddenly and pretend to be the housemaid?

'Abby, say something,' Sylvia demanded sharply. 'I know it's you, so there's no use hanging up or pretending it isn't.'

Abby sighed. She'd given Ethan her word that she wouldn't tell Sylvia about their arrangement, but she could hardly have anticipated this. Lying seemed stupid at this stage.

'Yes, Sylvia, it's me,' she said, resignation in her voice.

'What on earth are you doing down there...at Bungarla...in Ethan's room?'

'Being a good little employee,' Abby replied ruefully. For the time being, that was. Abby now accepted that

83

she could never work for Ethan ever again after this. The thought depressed her unbearably, but it had to be.

'I'm sorry, but I . . . I don't understand.'

'You only have yourself to blame, Sylvia. You put the idea into Ethan's head.'

'What idea?'

'Hiring a female escort for the conference. Last Friday night, after you left, he offered to pay me to come with him and I agreed.'

'He did? You *did*?'

Abby smiled wryly at Sylvia's startled bewilderment. 'You don't have to sound so shocked, Sylvia. It's merely a business arrangement. Nothing to get all het up about.'

'But you're in his *room*!'

'We have separate sleeping arrangements,' she said firmly, glancing at the sofa which she'd been relieved to find *did* unfold into a second bed. God knows what she'd have done if it hadn't.

'I see,' Sylvia said slowly. 'Yes, I see. At least, I hope so.'

'There's no hanky-panky going on, if that's what you're thinking.'

'More's the pity.'

Abby was taken aback by both the remark and its dry tone. 'What on earth do you mean by that?'

'Is Ethan there with you now?'

'He's in the shower. We're going down for pre-dinner drinks at six.' Just thirty minutes away. Abby wasn't looking forward to it.

'Then I must speak quickly. Ethan never spends long in the shower. He would also kill me if he knew I was about to tell you this, but I've been so worried since coming into the office this afternoon and finding that letter on Ethan's desk.'

Abby had a pretty good idea of what letter Sylvia was talking about, but decided not to let on. As much as Abby had tried not to be curious about Ethan's past relationship with the Ballistrats, she was. So she was eager to hear what Sylvia had to say about the matter.

'Lord, but this is difficult,' Sylvia muttered. 'I'll just have to be blunt. Look, about ten years ago, when Ethan was a resident, he fell in love with a nurse—a gorgeous-looking blonde named Vanessa. They moved in together and were going to be married. In fact the wedding was only a couple of weeks away when she ran off with another doctor—a famous visiting neurosurgeon named Dr Philip Ballistrat. You must have heard of him. Maybe you even heard of the scandal at the time. The man was married with a family. The wife was very vocal and bitter.'

'Yes, I do recall the incident,' she murmured, feeling a lot of sympathy for the youthful Ethan, but little for him now. To be jilted like that was not nice, but the man should have put it all behind him by now, not remained bitter and twisted for all these years.

'Of course, nobody paid any attention to the young doctor she left behind, but Ethan was devastated,' Sylvia explained with sisterly understanding. 'Simply devastated. He was crazy about her, and she'd seemed to be crazy about him. I worried for his sanity and his life for a long time after she left. I thought he might go after her and do something . . . well . . . something silly . . .

'But he didn't, thank God. Dr Ballistrat went overseas to America, where he took up some post at a big fancy clinic which charges huge fees. He's never been back to Australia. Till now. He's going to be at the conference, Abby. Lecturing. Which means *Vanessa's* going to be there too. I'm positive the only reason Ethan changed his mind about going was because of that, and I'm afraid of what he might do.'

'Ethan is not a violent man, Sylvia,' Abby assured the worried woman.

'No, I know he's not.'

'And this all happened *years* ago!' she exclaimed with some exasperation.

'Maybe so, but he's never forgotten or forgiven. I've always felt there was something about their break-up which Ethan never told me—something really wicked on her part, something totally unforgivable.'

'Such as what?'

'I don't know. All I know is that Ethan's up to something. Maybe he's not about to do murder, but what if he's planning to steal Vanessa back from Philip Ballistrat as a type of revenge? He was besotted with that woman once. Maybe he still is, in a way.'

Abby could hear the panic rising in Sylvia's voice. The woman was getting herself in a real tizzy. 'Now, why would he have gone to the trouble of hiring *me* to be by his side if his intention was wife-stealing?' she argued reasonably. 'No, Sylvia, I don't believe that for one moment. I think he just wants to see her again, that's all. But he didn't want *her* seeing *him* without an attractive young woman on his arm. He has his pride, you know. I don't believe Ethan's about to do anything stupid. He's just laying an old ghost to rest.'

'Oh, I do hope you're right and I'm wrong. I just have this awful feeling. I know you said your being with Ethan was just a business arrangement, but please, Abby, do your best to keep him right away from that woman, will you? She's poison where Ethan's concerned. And who knows? Now that he's older, and very successful, Vanessa might decide to give her ageing husband the flick and go for Ethan again. That's less likely to happen if the lovely girl by his side uses some of her previously understated attractions to distract him, don't you think?'

'What, exactly, are you proposing, Sylvia?' Abby asked slowly.

'You know exactly what I'm proposing, Abby,' came back the forthright remark. 'You're not that naïve. Frankly, when I first hired you I secretly hoped something might develop between you and Ethan. *And* I think he knew it, the stubborn, cantankerous devil! Why else would he have gone to so much trouble to keep you at a safe distance? All that "Miss Richmond" rubbish didn't fool me one bit.

'And you're just as bad,' she swept on before Abby could open her mouth. 'I know that underneath everything you find Ethan attractive. What woman wouldn't? So don't bother to deny it. All I'm suggesting is that now you're in a more intimate situation don't do anything to stop nature taking its natural course. You might even give it a helping hand, so to speak.'

'Ethan doesn't like women who fawn all over him,' she said drily.

'Then don't fawn. Flirt.'

'Flirt?'

'Yes. Believe me, Vanessa will. She's the expert of experts when it comes to flirting. Wait till you see her in action.'

Abby was in no hurry to see Vanessa at all, let alone flirting with Ethan. The very thought made her insides go all tight. Surely Ethan wouldn't have anything to do with a woman like that again. Surely not!

The shower water being switched off made her jump.

'Ethan's finished in the shower, Sylvia,' she whispered hurriedly. 'I think, if you don't want him knowing about this conversation, you'd better hang up. I also won't mention you rang.'

'You'll do what I asked, then?'

Abby swallowed. 'I . . . I'll do my best.'

'Oh, thank you, thank you. I've been sick with worry.'

'I'm not going to sleep with him, Sylvia. That's asking too much.'

'Only do what you feel comfortable with, dear,' Ethan's sister said rather smugly, and hung up.

Abby grimaced as she replaced the receiver and hurried back to where she'd been doing her hair.

Lord, what a pickle! Hired by the brother to be a pretend lover, then urged by the sister to become a real one—neither of them knowing how she actually felt about the man. If it wasn't so damned dangerous a situation, it would be funny!

Abby wanted to help Sylvia out, but really it was impossible. If she started flirting with Ethan after the way she'd just carried on, he'd wonder what on earth was happening. Either that, or he'd cynically think that she was after more money for extra-curricular activities, and would probably take her up in what she seemed to be offering.

Abby didn't believe that her cold-hearted boss was in anyway smitten with her, but he was a man, after all. And a man who didn't have too many qualms about where he got his sex—which might include with his silly receptionist!

That was all very well for him. He could obviously bed a woman he didn't love without turning a hair. As much as Abby had toughened up during her four-year stint in prison, she didn't think she was tough enough to make love with Ethan and walk away afterwards totally unscathed.

It was the first time Abby had conceded that she might feel a fraction more for Ethan than just lust. Only a fraction, mind. But it was enough to worry the hell out of her. She'd been brutally used by one man in her life and she wasn't about to set herself up to be used by another.

So she wisely decided not to make even the slightest flirtatious move till she saw the lie of the land for herself. For all she knew, it might not be necessary for her to 'distract' Ethan in any way at all. Vanessa might take one look at him and not give him a second glance, and vice versa.

The bathroom door opened and Ethan walked out, naked except for a large fluffy cream towel looped casually around his waist. His black hair was still wet from the shower, and a few wayward locks flopped rakishly across his high forehead. The dark curls in the centre of his chest were also still damp, tight little swirls of glistening hair which screamed out to have a woman's fingers slide sensually through them.

Abby did her best not to stare, her heart sinking all the while. Vanessa would definitely take a second glance. She was taking more than two herself.

'Was that the telephone just now?' he asked abruptly.

She swallowed and lifted her eyes back to his face, praying that nothing showed in her expression or demeanour to betray her X-rated thoughts. 'No,' she lied fairly smoothly.

'Must have been next door,' he muttered, scooping the now dripping locks back from his forehead with both hands, the action highlighting muscles in his chest and arms which hadn't come from lifting a scalpel. Either he worked out regularly with weights, or he'd been born with a physique most men had to sweat long hours for.

'Won't be long,' he added, then strode back into the bathroom without looking at her again.

Abby let out a shuddering sigh. 'Take all the time you like, Ethan,' she murmured. 'I'm in no hurry.'

But it seemed Ethan *was*, for less than five minutes later he emerged from the bathroom a second time. Thankfully he was fully dressed this time, though he still looked devastatingly attractive in elegant black trousers and an open-necked burgundy-coloured shirt which had fullish sleeves. He was combing his hair as he walked, trying to put some order into his still wet black waves.

'I think I should have had a haircut before I came,' he grumbled.

Abby disagreed. Longish, his hair was wildly attractive and compellingly touchable. Combined with his naturally olive complexion and that shirt, his overall look tonight was gypsyish and sinfully sexy.

When he glanced up to find her standing stock-still and staring at him, she adopted a casually thoughtful expression, as though she was studying his hair at his behest. 'Actually, it suits you long,' she said carelessly.

'I see you've put *your* hair up again,' he returned.

Abby shrugged, though the thought crossed her mind that if things looked really bad where the awful Vanessa was concerned, she might leave it down a couple of times. From experience, leaving her hair down invariably drew male attention, and Ethan had already expressed a desire to see it down. Such a gesture would be more subtle than openly flirting with him.

'You *are* going to be ready in time, aren't you?' he demanded brusquely, scowling at her still robed body.

'I only have to slip into my clothes.' And put my lipstick on, plus my perfume, not to mention my jewellery, she added silently.

'Then do so. I promised Henry I would collect them right on six.'

He was tense, Abby saw. Very tense. Because of Vanessa, no doubt. Presumably he hoped to see her during the cocktail hour, when people tended to mingle.

Abby extracted her chosen clothes from where she'd hung them in the wardrobe, scooped up the velvet case which contained her pearls and hurried into the bathroom.

She took only two minutes to slip into the classically tailored blue suit and cream satin camisole, another thirty seconds to apply the coral lipstick which matched the coral nail polish she'd painted on earlier, then another few seconds to spray a conservative amount of Miss Blanchford's Chanel No. 5 behind her ears and on her wrists. Abby finally dropped the long single rope of pearls over her neck, then clipped the pearl drops to her lobes.

Sylvia would be pleased, she thought wryly as she surveyed her reflection, aware that the outfit looked more provocative on her than she recalled it looking five years ago. Those few extra inches on her figure again.

The camisole was not overly low-cut, but its shoelace straps precluded her wearing a bra. The pearl necklace had settled into the shadowed valley between her unfettered breasts, bringing attention to the beginnings of a cleavage. Cheap and flashy she was not, but there was no denying it was an eyecatching outfit.

Abby frowned at the tightness of the straight skirt around her hips and bottom, wishing she'd had more time to lose just a little more weight. Thank heaven the jacket reached down a fair way, and also covered her suspiciously erect nipples.

Sighing at her silly self, she pulled a few extra strands of hair out of the loose chignon to curl around her face and neck, thinking that they might soften the image she presented. But she ended up looking even more sexy, as though she'd been kissing her lover and he'd tangled his hands in her hair.

God! She almost stamped her foot in frustration.

An impatient tap on the door had her yanking it open and striding out, defiant eyes flying to Ethan.

'I'm almost ready,' she snapped. 'I only have to slip into my shoes. It's only five to six, you know.' She jammed her stockinged feet into cream court shoes with finely pointed heels. A year or two ago they would have been hopelessly out of fashion, but the style had come back in, thank heavens.

'There. I'm done. Do I pass?' she asked, striking a model's pose for him. She knew she was being a bit of a bitch, but fear of making a fool of herself had drawn her nerves tight.

Ethan's gaze was irritatingly unreadable as he looked her up and down. 'You'll do,' he said, then strolled over to inspect the pearl necklace more closely. 'They look real.' He picked up the end and dangled it from his middle finger.

'They are,' she retorted, piqued by his attitude. He could have said something nice instead of being nasty. '*Everything* about me is real.'

His eyes turned sardonic as they moved over her breasts. 'Impressive,' came his droll remark before he dropped the pearls back into place, seemingly making a point of not actually touching her. 'So is your wardrobe, by the look of things. My three thousand might have covered the clothes, not to mention the undoubtedly expensive perfume which is wafting from your delectable body, but I'd say it would be struggling to stretch to the price of those pearls. So tell me, Abigail...where does a casually employed working girl get the money to buy real pearls?'

'Not from my pathetic salaries, I can assure you,' she countered scornfully. A minute ago she might have told him the truth, but not now. Why give him the opportunity to hold her in more contempt by not believing her. 'They were gifts,' she said offhandedly.

'From men?'

'No. Just one man.' It wasn't even a lie. Her father had paid for all her clothes, and her mother's gifts had really been bought with her father's money as well.

'Ah. So that's the answer to what you were doing before you came to work for me. You had a sugar-daddy. I suppose he's the one who paid for you to go overseas as well. Sylvia says you've travelled extensively over the past few years.'

'That's right.'

'How old was he, this man who showered you with gifts and trips?'

'How old?' she retorted, swallowing.

'It's a simple question, Abigail. How old was this man?'

Abby gulped again. She hadn't meant this petty little word-game of hers to go this far. 'That's none of your business,' she tossed back, and went to walk past him.

His hand shot out and grabbed her upper arm, swinging her round. 'How old?' he rasped down into her face.

The pain shooting through her arm brought another spurt of defiant anger. 'A lot older than you,' she spat at him. 'And a hell of a lot richer!'

He let her go, his blue eyes like chips of ice.

'I can't believe how disappointed in you I am,' he drawled. 'There I was, thinking I might have misjudged you.'

'Really? Well, I'm not disappointed in you, Ethan,' she returned frostily. 'Because I never misjudged *you*.'

'Meaning?'

'I don't think we have time for a deep and meaningful chat about our respective weaknesses, do you? But be assured, my relationship with this man was based on love, not lust.'

'You mean he loved you?' Ethan said derisively.

'No, I mean *I* loved *him*. As it turned out, he didn't love me at all.'

Ethan was obviously taken aback. His frown betrayed surprise, then a dark thoughtfulness. 'But you don't love him any more.'

'I wish I didn't.'

'Are you saying you still *do*?' Ethan sounded angry with her.

She could see his point, but how did one stop loving a parent? She even loved her mother—her silly, feckless, selfish mother. 'I dare say I'll always love him,' she confessed, her heart turning over.

'But that's stupid,' he snapped. 'The man used you, can't you see that?'

Abby found a measure of relief for poor Sylvia's concern in Ethan's words. If that was his way of thinking then he clearly no longer loved Vanessa. Unless it was a case of do as I say, not as I do. Men had a tendency to hypocrisy in matters of love and sex.

'I can see more than you give me credit for, Ethan,' she bit out. 'Now, no more talk about the past, please. It's gone and should stay gone. It's also gone six, and Henry and Ann will be waiting. Shall we go?'

CHAPTER NINE

ANN was looking pretty in pink silk, with Henry quite suave in a polo-necked jumper and tweedish smoking jacket. The two couples were moving along the covered walkway which led from the motel-style units back to the main building of the hotel when Ethan startled Abby by sliding an arm around her waist.

'For appearances' sake,' he whispered wryly into her ear as he pulled her close.

Abby stiffened beneath his touch. God, but she could actually feel the heat of his palm right through her jacket and skirt. Or was it her own sudden heat she was feeling, the heat of a burning sexual awareness? Whatever, she quivered inside when his fingers splayed over the curve of her hip, thrilling to the way they applied a masterful pressure as he steered her through the doorway into the hotel.

She'd always admired Ethan's hands, with their long, elegant fingers and economically graceful movements. But she'd never guessed how strong they were. How strong *he* was. Seeing him semi-naked had shown her an Ethan other than the coolly professional surgeon she encountered every Friday afternoon. The memory sent more heat through her body, travelling with speed around her veins to every tiny capillary, making her feel hot all over.

'This way,' Henry said, directing them to the hallway which would bring them back to the front lobby. 'Reception actually gave me a map of the hotel with all the rooms marked for all the various functions, so we poor, unintelligent medicos don't get lost. Did they give you one, Ethan?'

'Probably. They gave me a whole pile of stuff which I threw on the coffee-table. I haven't really had time to look at it yet.'

'Oh? What on earth have you two been doing for the past two hours, old chap?'

Abby felt Ethan's fingers freeze on her flesh.

'None of your business, Henry,' he said evenly.

'Henry,' Ann warned.

'All right, all right. I'll be good. Truly, I'm sure Abby wasn't offended. You weren't, were you, Abby love?'

'Not at all,' Abby admitted, despite her cheeks feeling awfully hot.

'There. I knew she wouldn't be. Not like that Madam Muck you brought to dinner a month or so ago, Ethan.'

'Oh, God!' Ann exclaimed exasperatedly. 'Do shut up, Henry, before you put your other foot in your mouth as well.'

Henry genuinely looked perplexed. 'What did I say that was so wrong?'

'Abby doesn't want to hear about Ethan's other women,' Ann snapped.

'It's all right, Henry,' Abby reassured him. 'I know all about Ethan's other women—Evelyn included. Ethan and I are very open with each other, aren't we, darling?'

The 'darling' just slipped out before she could stop it. Ethan arched a cold eyebrow down at her, at the same time digging his fingertips into her hip. His smile was quite frightening, if one was accustomed to its chilling undertones.

'Too true,' he agreed in a low, silkily menacing voice. 'There's nothing I don't know about Abigail, here. Absolutely nothing.'

Abby resisted pulling a face at him. God, but he was a cynical bastard. Why she wanted him so much she had no idea. 'Oh, I wouldn't go that far, darling,' she countered, finding sweet revenge in not dropping the endearment. 'A woman wouldn't be a woman if she didn't have some little secrets.' And mine are real whoppers! she thought.

For a split second Abby felt a frisson of fear that someone here might know about her stay in prison. But she quickly dismissed it again as highly unlikely. She couldn't see too many surgeons showing up with ex-cons as wives or even girlfriends.

'Secrets are not the sole prerogative of women,' Henry announced heartily. 'I know a few doctors who practically lead a double life when it comes to their pursuit of the opposite sex! Up the stairs here, folks. Cocktails are being served on the first floor.'

'Don't look at me, Ann,' Ethan defended himself. 'I'm too damned busy to bother with juggling women. One woman at a time is more than enough for me. Especially one like Abigail. She's such a loving little thing, aren't you, darling?'

When Abby automatically glanced up at this mocking return of the endearment, he stunned her by bending down and kissing her on the lips.

It was over almost before it began, a mere brushing of mouth against mouth. But oh, how it sent her heart a-thudding and her eyes a-widening. She stared up at him as his head lifted, knowing that if he ever chose to leave those lips on hers for longer than two miserable seconds, she would be in deep, deep trouble.

His blue eyes narrowed as he frowned back down into her stunned face. Was he reading her troubled and very vulnerable mind? Already planning a ruthless seduction, perhaps?

The possibility was perversely delicious to think about, but Abby knew that such a reality would be a disaster. She knew who would be the one who ended up getting hurt, and it wouldn't be Mr Hyde.

'Enough of that for now,' Ann interrupted. 'There's just so much spontaneous passion I can stand on an empty stomach. I'll let you continue canoodling after I've had a couple of G and Ts.'

'We'll await your permission with bated breath,' Ethan said with another rueful glance down at Abby. 'Lead on, Henry. I think I could do with a drink myself.'

Me, too, Abby agreed. Alcohol had a tendency to make her aggressive and sarcastic, not at all the mellow you-can-do-anything-you-like-with-me type of female most men hoped for when they plied their partner with drink. Dillon had taken some time to realise that he did much better with chocolates and compliments than wine.

Not that Abby seriously thought that Ethan was interested in getting her drunk, or in seducing her. He was just being his usual supercilious self, trying to niggle her. It was a continuation of the coldly competitive game of one-upmanship they'd played with each other right from the first day.

'Straight ahead,' Henry directed, ushering Ann towards the open doorway directly opposite the top of the stairs.

The first room they entered contained a large centrally located bar and a polished wooden rectangular construction with a black leather top and a myriad of matching stools anchored to the red carpet on steel poles.

The rest of the large room was filled with groupings of armchairs and tables, most of which were occupied. A smoke haze filled the air, which caused Ann immediately to wrinkle her nose.

'Clearly this is the smoking section,' she said. 'But I see an archway over there and clear air in the distance. Come on. Let's find our pure lungs a more suitable breathing place for the next hour.'

Abby couldn't help but notice the way Ethan looked around as they followed Ann and Henry through the smoke-filled room, his searching gaze checking out every group of people, including those sitting and standing at the bar. Was he looking for Vanessa? she wondered. And felt an irritating pang of jealousy.

Several of the men greeted him by name, their women companions invariably looking him up and down—all with interest, some with outright hunger. Abby found herself glaring back at these with open hostility. She even linked arms with him at one stage, staking her pretend possession. It brought a sour glance from Ethan and a muttered, 'Don't overdo it.'

'You started it,' she returned airily. 'You should never have kissed me like that. I was overcome.'

'I did notice you were stunned into silence for a second or two.'

'Shock does rather have that effect on one.'

'Hopefully, next time I kiss you you won't look quite so much like a stunned mullet.'

'*Next* time?' she repeated, her stomach flipping over at the thought.

'Having established your highly affectionate nature, it seems only natural that I would act differently with you from my usual distant self.'

'Stop whispering you two,' Ann said, glancing over her shoulder at them. Her gaze moved momentarily beyond Ethan and Abby, her eyes suddenly flinging wide. She stopped walking, tugging on Henry's sleeve as she did so. 'It's her, Henry,' she gasped. 'The hussy! She's just walked in. And alone too. Don't turn round, Ethan. Pretend you're talking to me while I surreptitiously watch.'

Ethan didn't turn round, but his spine had gone instantly ramrod-straight, the hand on Abby's hip freezing. Abby risked a peek over her shoulder. The hussy Ann was referring to was Vanessa Ballistrat, all right, looking exquisitely feminine in oyster pearl chiffon.

'I presume you're referring to Mrs Ballistrat,' Abby said in a superbly bland voice.

'Don't tell me you know of her, Abby? Why, you're much too young to remember the scandal when it happened.'

'Actually, I do remember it. Quite well. I was at boarding school at the time, and my girlfriends and I used to devour all the women's magazines. I even remember her first name. It was Vanessa. But I like hussy much better. It suits her. She hasn't changed all that much, physically speaking, has she?' she remarked, with another glance over her shoulder at the blonde, who'd already been claimed by a male admirer.

'I'd say she was *better* looking, if anything,' Ann remarked sourly. 'And still obviously irresistible to men.'

Ethan stayed standing like a statue, his face grim, his fingers now like ice. Abby tried to feel sympathy for him. Instead, all she felt was a fierce frustration, and more curiosity than ever.

'Did you and Henry know her personally back then, Ann?' she went on, determined to bring as much out in the open as she dared. 'Ethan tells me she used to work at the hospital where he was a resident.'

'Is that so?' Henry commented interestedly. 'Would that I had been so lucky, but I worked in Canberra around that time. What was she like, Ethan?'

'Irresistible to men,' Ethan said drily.

Henry laughed. 'Not you too, old chap. I heard from an American doctor I know that she takes scalps wherever she goes. When we read that letter, cock-crowing about this conference having ensnared old Ballistrat as a lecturer, Ann and I were curious to see for ourselves exactly what he risked his career for. I must say that even from this distance she packs quite a punch. Marilyn Monroe reincarnated, with a touch of Marlene Dietrich thrown in for good measure. Mmm, yes... ve—ry nice indeed.'

Ethan at last turned to see for himself, his hand falling away from Abby's hip as he did so. She should have felt relieved by this. Instead, she felt oddly bereft. Abandoned. Rejected. She wanted his hand back on her flesh, wanted the intimacy—however slight—sustained.

She stared up at him, troubled by the emotion racing through her, hating the time he was taking in surveying his old flame.

Whilst Ethan's face remained fairly impassive, Abby thought she glimpsed a tightening around his mouth and a darkening in his eyes as he watched the woman. By the time he turned back to face them, she found that she was holding her breath.

'You're right, Ann,' he drawled, his tone bored. 'She *is* better looking. But I doubt she's changed in other ways. Let's go and get ourselves a drink. My throat's as dry as the Simpson Desert.' Taking Abby's arm, he urged her forward, forcing his friends to move on.

Abby slanted him a quick look, but there was nothing for her to see now. Clearly Ethan was a master at hiding his feelings once he put his mind to it.

Did he still want Vanessa? she agonised. Had he taken one look and been swamped by renewed desire for her beautiful face and body? They'd been lovers once, had *lived* together, for pity's sake! She had probably made love like a sex goddess, knowing exactly what Ethan had wanted and needed to make him happy. Sylvia had said he'd been devastated when she'd left him, her power over him so strong that he'd almost gone mad with losing her. He might hate her, but he still wanted her. Abby felt sure of it.

God, but she'd never felt so jealous of a woman in all her life! It was a telling moment, and one which Abby struggled to explain to herself—unfortunately not with a satisfactory answer. All she knew was that she was going to do everything possible to keep that bitch away from Ethan.

The second lounge was smaller, quieter and very comfy, with a couple of waiters circling the room and offering drinks and hors d'oeuvres to the occupants.

They settled into a corner, Ethan drawing Abby down with him into a deep two-seater against the wall and Ann and Henry pulling up armchairs, forming a U-shaped group which didn't prevent anyone from looking around the room or through the wide archway into the bar beyond. Abby wondered if Ethan had chosen the spot for that reason, so he could keep an eye on Vanessa. It seemed likely, considering this was why he had come.

Once everyone was seated, one of the hovering waiters immediately offered them a large selection of drinks from an oval silver tray. Abby took a glass of champagne,

Ann a dry sherry, Henry a beer and Ethan a Scotch and water.

'I wonder where her doting husband is tonight?' Henry resumed, obviously not willing to let the subject of Vanessa drop. Hard to do when she was in full view, standing with a group just through the archway.

A group of *men*, Abby noted ruefully. She had her hand on one of the men's arms and was smiling up at him as though what he was saying was simply riveting.

'Perhaps he isn't feeling well,' Ethan said, and curled his free arm around Abby's shoulders. She glanced up at him before producing what she hoped was her best 'come hither' smile. Anything to stop him looking at that woman. He blinked for a moment, then smiled back, a slow, sardonic curve which might have seemed seductively warm to anyone who only knew Dr Jekyll and not Mr Hyde.

'You'll keep,' he murmured in so low a voice that only she could hear, his lips pressed against her hair.

'What do you mean, Ethan?' Henry persisted. 'What do you know that I don't know about Ballistrat?'

'I don't know how much you know, Henry, but rumour has it he has some form of arthritis in his fingers and can't operate any more. That's why he's been reduced to the lecture tour circuit. They say he has money troubles and is drinking like a fish as well. Maybe he's not here for cocktails because he doesn't dare—in case he has a hangover tomorrow.'

Abby absorbed all this information with growing concern. Ethan had certainly gone to a lot of trouble to find out about Dr Ballistrat. She was sure that he hadn't known any of this last Friday, when that letter had arrived. Sylvia could be right about Ethan planning some sort of revenge. Not necessarily violent, but maybe just as vindictive. The objective of that revenge didn't seem to be Vanessa, however, but the man who'd stolen her from him.

'I wouldn't take too many bets on that marriage lasting, then,' Henry said. 'Women like Blondie like the good things in life. And I wouldn't rank being poor in that category.'

Too true, Abby thought caustically.

'Well, well,' Henry said with gleeful anticipation. 'Our luck's in. She's coming this way. You might be able to introduce us, Ethan. Why don't you wave her over?'

Abby watched the hussy enter the room with the man whose arm she'd been clinging to. Immediately she felt not only inferior in the beauty stakes, but a great big clumsy horse by comparison.

The woman didn't walk, she floated—the chiffon skirt swirling sensuously about her slender legs. She was really quite tiny, with a pocket Venus figure, a creamy, unlined complexion and the shiniest blonde hair Abby had ever seen. The colour of whipped cream, it curved around her face in soft waves, its glossy paleness a perfect foil for her eyes which were large and limpid and blue. *Very* blue. The bluest of blue lagoons against the whitest of white sand.

Abby could well imagine any man drowning in them.

They all watched her approach, every single one of them, with various expressions written on their faces. Henry with goggled-eyed admiration; Ann with avid curiosity; Abby with envy and Ethan with far too studied an indifference, Abby thought. He didn't fool her one bit. She could feel his tension through the arm around her shoulders.

Vanessa didn't appear to notice them watching her, keeping her big blue eyes glued to the man she was with, seemingly wrapped in what he was saying.

Abby recognised the act for what it was. An act. The beautiful Mrs Ballistrat wasn't at all interested in what her companion was saying. What she cared about was the admiration she was getting in return. Abby had known the type before. Women who thrived on male attention, could not live without it. Her own mother had been one.

Suddenly Vanessa laughed, a caressing feminine sound which held promise of the sweetest of natures.

'What an actress!' Ann muttered disgruntledly, obviously thinking the same thoughts as Abby.

Henry chuckled. 'Who cares? She can turn those big baby blues on me any time she likes.'

'Over my dead body,' Ann snorted.

'I wouldn't say that too loudly, if I were you, Ann,' Ethan remarked, a sardonic edge to his voice. 'Women like Vanessa would not stop at murder to get any man they wanted.'

'I believe you,' Ann returned sourly.

'Hush up, you two,' Henry muttered. 'She's coming over here.'

Which she was, having dispensed with her companion, who stood staring longingly after her, looking both adoring and crushed. But he was no longer wanted—hadn't been from the moment the hussy had spotted Ethan out of the corner of her eye.

She floated towards their corner, her gaze clamped to Ethan's face. She didn't seem at all surprised to see him there, though a degree of apprehension did cloud her beautiful blue eyes as she drew closer, as though she was unsure of her welcome. Her wariness grew as she drew to a slightly nervous halt in front of him, a red-nailed and very feminine hand fluttering up to her throat.

'Hello, Ethan,' she said softly. 'It's been a long time. *Too* long,' she added, her melodic voice carrying real regret.

'You're looking remarkably well, Vanessa,' Ethan returned with surprising charm. 'Would you care to join us for a drink?'

Ann looked daggers at him, Abby noted, but he ignored her. I'd like to kill him myself, she thought mutinously. True to form, Henry was delighted, jumping to his feet immediately. 'I'll pull up a chair for you.'

Vanessa beamed at him. 'Oh, thank you. What a nice man you are,' she added sweetly, as he slid a chair into the gap between his and Ann's, completing a cosy little circle.

Vanessa sank gracefully into it, the chiffon skirt making a swishing sound as she delicately crossed her legs. Her eyes immediately returned to Ethan's, as though they held some secret magnet for her. 'I was so surprised when I saw your name on the register, Ethan,' she said, smiling her pleasure. 'Not that I should have been. You always said you'd become a top orthopaedic surgeon. I'll bet you're good.'

'I like to think I am,' Ethan returned modestly.

'He's more than good,' Henry inserted. 'He's the best bone man in Australia, even if he is the rudest. Since Ethan's forgotten his manners, we'll introduce ourselves. Dr Henry Maclean at your service, Mrs Ballistrat.'

'Oh, do call me Vanessa,' she said, leaning over and touching him lightly on the wrist. 'I can't abide formality.' With the leaning forward, her high and impossibly perfect breasts formed a deep cleavage within the low V-neckline of her dress.

Henry only just managed not to gawk. 'You won't get any arguments from me on that score,' he said, his florid face gaining some more redness.

'And I'm Ann Maclean,' Ann said coldly. 'Henry's wife.'

'How do you do, Mrs Maclean?' came the equally cool reply. Clearly formality still applied to wives.

Abby waited for those big blue eyes to turn to her, which they eventually did, but only after lingering on Ethan again for a few more moments. Abby couldn't catch Ethan's reaction without being obvious.

'And I dare say this sweet young thing is Mrs Ethan Grant?' she suggested.

Abby cringed at the description, and the woman's saccharine tone.

'Not as yet, Vanessa,' Ethan returned, before Abby could think of a suitably cutting retort. 'But that's to be remedied shortly. I know we said we'd keep it a secret for a while yet, darling,' he murmured, giving Abby an affectionate squeeze, 'but what's the point? I asked Abby to marry me this afternoon and she bravely said yes.'

CHAPTER TEN

ABBY suspected that her eyes must have shown shock, but she doubted anyone saw it, Ethan immediately obliterating her face from view as his mouth swooped.

Shock quickly changed to resentment as he forced his will upon her lips, but resentment proved a poor weapon against the mad desire which was lurking deep within her treacherous body. How could she possibly keep her lips primly shut when Ethan's tongue was demanding entry? It was what she'd dreamt about, what she'd fantasised over.

So she opened her mouth and let him kiss her—*really* kiss her.

It was once again only a brief kiss. Even so, for those few savage seconds everything else ceased to exist. Where they were. Henry and Ann. Even the dreaded Vanessa.

Ethan's tongue surged deep into her mouth, tracing a swiftly erotic path around her own tongue, then up over the roof of her mouth. When it abruptly withdrew she almost moaned her disappointment, only then remembering where they were and who was watching.

Ann and Henry were smiling broadly at her blushing face, but Vanessa looked as if she was carved in stone. Abby still felt somewhat disorientated, but it did cross her muddled mind that Ethan's unexpected statement was part of his secret plan where that woman was concerned.

Had he been going to up her status all along? Or had it been a spur-of-the-moment decision, based on

Vanessa's reaction to him? If he thought his being engaged would discourage her, he was in for a surprise. The past showed that neither engagement ring nor wedding ring would stop the woman if she wanted someone.

And she wanted Ethan. Abby had no doubts about that any longer. But did he want her back?

Another thought struck, and Abby recoiled. Was she being used as a blind? Had Ethan planned on having an adulterous rendezvous with Vanessa all along? Maybe he did despise the woman, but still desperately desired her. Maybe her undoubted sexual prowess still haunted his dreams. Maybe the way he wanted to lay *this* ghost to rest was to lay her—literally...

Abby's eyes cleared to find Henry and Ann both congratulating them and castigating them for not telling them earlier.

'We weren't going to say anything till I could buy her a ring,' Ethan explained, hugging Abby to his side. Again. 'Aren't you going to congratulate us, Vanessa?'

'But of course,' she purred. 'I'm just surprised some lucky girl didn't snap you up long ago.'

'I doubt I've been suitable marriage material over the past ten years,' Ethan countered casually. 'You know what they say. All work and no play makes Jack a dull boy.'

'Not you, Ethan. You were never dull.'

'He surprised us too, Vanessa,' Henry chimed in. 'Even showing up here with Abby was a surprise. I didn't get a whiff of a serious romance from the sneaky devil, and I work with him three days a week.'

'Is that so?' The big blue eyes threw Abby a thoughtful glance.

Abby reacted automatically, her only objective to wipe that speculative look right off Vanessa's too beautiful face.

'Ethan likes to keep his private life, private, don't you, darling?' she murmured, gazing at him adoringly before lifting her mouth and pressing a soft little kiss on the corner of his mouth. 'Actually, we've been crazy about each other since the first day we met six months ago, but we took our time in revealing our true feelings. But once we did, all that pent-up emotion just sort of exploded!'

'Oh, how romantic!' Ann sighed.

The waiter returning to offer fresh drinks came as a welcome distraction at that point. He was quickly followed by a waitress carrying a huge tray of hors d'oeuvres.

Vanessa wasn't at all happy with the selection of either, and asked Henry if he would mind getting her a dry martini from the bar. Much to Ann's chagrin, he hopped up immediately and dashed off to do the blonde's bidding. Vanessa was fairly gushing in her gratitude on his return, making a big fuss of Henry's 'gentlemanly' qualities and bestowing the most outrageous compliments about his 'dashing' clothes.

Poor Henry. He was her slave from that moment. It seemed that with Ethan's declaration of imminent matrimony, plus his open display of affection for the woman by his side, a piqued Vanessa had temporarily switched her charm in another direction.

Ann looked positively livid, Ethan fell cryptically silent, and Abby wished that she was back in Sydney. Lord, what a mess she had got herself into. Here she was, actually wishing that she *was* engaged to the infuriating and unfathomable man crushed up against her.

Yet she didn't love him. She didn't even *like* him. She did, however, seem to care about what happened to him. God knows why! Maybe it had something to do with Sylvia, who was such a nice woman that one had to believe her brother must have some niceness in him somewhere too. Or maybe it was because she wanted an excuse to explore the very real pent-up emotion which had indeed been building up in her since she'd met the man.

Genuinely engaged people invariably made love these days, didn't they? When they shared a hotel room they didn't worry about whether the sofa unfolded into a second bed. They tumbled into the one double bed together, ripping off their clothes and urging their panting, naked bodies into one flesh without hesitation. The very thought of doing as much with Ethan sent her blood coursing hotly through her veins.

Abby shuddered as she recognised that her lust for Ethan was now in real danger of getting out of hand. She'd almost got to the stage where she didn't care about pride, or any of that self-respect rubbish. She wanted the man. Why couldn't she have him? What was to stop her?

He wouldn't knock her back.

Or would he? she frowned.

Maybe he would!

Now, that was one blow her pride could not take. To offer herself to Ethan Grant and have him reject her. The very thought made her feel nauseous. No, she could not—*would not*—put herself in such a humiliating position.

Another shudder rippled through her.

'Cold, darling?' Ethan murmured, wrapping his arm more tightly around her and pulling her even closer.

Abby gulped. My God, she'd be in his lap soon!

'No,' she denied, trying to extricate herself from his steely hold but failing. 'Well, maybe a little,' she said, and lanced him with a warning glare.

His returning smile mocked her discomfort. He knew that she was hating being this close to him. What he didn't know, however, was that she was dangerously turned on, not repulsed at all.

'Drink up your wine,' he urged, a coldly amused gleam in his eyes. 'That should warm you up.'

'I doubt it,' she muttered, knowing the effect alcohol had on her.

'So tell me, Ethan,' Vanessa interrupted sweetly. 'How's your sister these days? Did she ever get married, or is she still happy just playing mother to you?'

Once again, Abby could feel the stiffening of Ethan's muscles.

'Sylvia's been a wonderful sister to me, Vanessa,' he praised, and Abby felt quite proud of him. 'I don't know what I would have done without her after our parents were killed. But no, she's never married. I don't think she's ever wanted to. She lives a full life—going to the theatre and ballet and playing bridge.'

'And does she approve of *you* marrying? Or will she be jealous of Abby?'

Ethan laughed. '*Jealous*? Sylvia simply adores Abby. Actually, I think she had this in mind when she first hired her.'

'Abby *works* for you?' Vanessa asked with a sour surprise.

'Didn't I say she did? Yes, Abby's my receptionist. I must say it makes work a pleasure to come in and see her lovely face over the desk every day.'

Abby almost choked on her drink. He really was laying it on a bit thick, the lying devil!

But she loved it. There was something wickedly pleasurable in the deception all of a sudden. Seeing Madame de Pompadour's perfect lips purse into a prim expression was worth any pretence, however dangerous.

'Oh, darling,' she murmured, cuddling into Ethan's side. 'You say such lovely things.'

'He *does*?' Henry chortled. 'Must be a different chap from the man who terrorises all the theatre nurses, in that case. He barks at them something rotten.'

'He never barked at *me*,' Vanessa murmured coyly.

'No man would bark at you, Vanessa,' said a doting Henry.

Ann rolled her eyes and called a waiter over for a third sherry. Clearly she was in dire need of another drink in the face of her husband's sickening display. Abby swallowed up her champagne and took another glass as well.

She had a feeling that she might need some alcohol-induced sarcasm later, if stupid bloody Henry asked Vanessa to join them for dinner. It would undoubtedly ruin her appetite, but hopefully not her tongue. Ethan might be the terror of the operating theatre, but *she* had been the terror of the prison laundry. If madam there thought she could get the better of Abby when it came to words, then she had another think coming!

As it turned out, Henry did ask her to join them for dinner, but—luckily for Vanessa—she had to decline. Apparently hubby was joining her for the actual meal, and they were expected to sit with the other lecturers. Abby almost felt disappointed that she wouldn't have the opportunity to sharpen her claws on the woman.

Ann, however, did not feel the same. 'Don't you ever, *ever* ask that bitch to join us again, Henry Maclean,' she hissed as soon as the woman was out of earshot.

Henry chortled, then leant over to give his wife a kiss on the cheek. 'I love it when you're jealous.'

'How you can be fooled by that man-eating tigress is beyond me!'

'I thought she was very engaging,' Henry huffed.

'So's the Venus fly-trap!' Ann spat.

And that was how it continued, all through dinner. Henry and Ann sparring, and Abby amused by Ann's tart remarks, which she privately agreed with.

Abby would have enjoyed the meal more if Ethan hadn't been so silent. The food was mouth-watering, the dining-room elegantly luxurious, the service splendid. It had been a long time since she'd eaten so well, and she forgot all about her intention to watch her weight, attacking each course with relish.

Afterwards, they sat over several cups of coffee for some time, till Ann started yawning.

'Tired, love?' Henry asked straight away.

'Rather. It's been a long day, what with driving the kids over to your mother's at God knows what hour this morning.'

'How about a nightcap at the bar, then we'll call it a night?' Henry suggested.

'All right,' Ann sighed.

Ethan happily agreed to Henry's suggestion. Abby had no objections either. But, as luck would have it, there was Vanessa, perched up at the bar on a stool, with another male admirer glued to her.

Where on earth was her husband? Abby fumed. Why didn't he lock her up and give all the poor, unsuspecting males in the world a break?

'Oh, dear,' Ann said when Vanessa swivelled round on the stool just in time to catch sight of their entry.

The smile she sent Ethan's way was inviting and seductive. 'She's like a cobweb. You can't brush her off.'

'Don't you mean a Black Widow spider?' Abby said, unable to resist a barb of her own.

'You could be right, girls,' Henry said as he feasted his eyes upon Vanessa's blatant show of leg. 'I reckon once she's finished with a man, he'll be a spent force. In the interests of matrimonial harmony, I think Ann and I will have our nightcap back in our room.'

Abby glanced hopefully up at Ethan, waiting for him to agree, but it seemed that scuttling off to his room was not part of his plan for this weekend—whatever that plan was. Abby was becoming increasingly irritated at being left in the dark.

'Fair enough, Henry,' Ethan said. 'Off you go. See you in the morning.'

Henry and Ann exchanged surprised glances before shrugging and departing for their room, leaving Abby feeling confused and dismayed. How could she keep Ethan away from the hussy if he actively sought out her company? Already he was guiding her over to the bar. Worse, the man Vanessa had been talking to was walking away at the same time, leaving an empty stool beside her.

'Mind if we join you for a nightcap?' Ethan said casually.

Her beautiful blue eyes flicked rather coldly over Abby before warming upon her preferred subject. 'Not at all,' she gushed. 'I was hoping you'd come over.'

Ethan guided Abby onto the empty stool, standing behind her with his hands curled rather possessively over her shoulders. She tried to relax under his intimate touch but found herself sitting stiffly, her face just as frozen.

Vanessa arched an eyebrow at her obvious discomfort, then proceeded to exert every ounce of her considerable charm on the man who'd once been her lover.

'I can't believe how marvellous you look, Ethan,' she complimented him. 'Not that you weren't always a handsome man. But you look so fit as well. A lot of professional men let themselves go, which is such a shame—don't you think so, dear?' she directed towards Abby, in a simperingly insincere voice.

Unfortunately, Abby could hardly do anything but agree.

'You've certainly looked after *yourself*, Vanessa,' Ethan pointed out. 'You haven't aged a day.'

Her smile carried satisfaction. 'How kind of you to say so. But you always were a flatterer, darling.'

'Not at all,' Ethan denied smoothly. 'I've always said it as it is.'

'Yes...yes, so you have.' She gave him a wistful look, full of longing. 'It really is lovely to see you again, Ethan. I've thought of you so many times over the years.'

'And I you, Vanessa.'

Abby's cheeks flamed with embarrassment and resentment. How dared Ethan conduct a nostalgic flirtation with this woman in her presence? She felt the urge to get up and walk out on both of them, but no sooner did the thought come into her head than Ethan's fingers increased the pressure on her shoulders, virtually holding her down on the stool by force.

Clearly he'd read her mind, and was reminding her to keep doing what she'd been paid to do, not indulge in hysterically emotional reactions.

But Abby couldn't seem to help it. Was it jealousy rampaging through her veins? Or just injured pride? She bitterly resented the feeling of being used, of being a pawn pushed this way and that without having any say in or knowledge of what was going on.

The hovering barman finally asked what they'd like to drink, and Vanessa ordered a cognac.

'Ethan, you'll have a cognac too, won't you?' she said. 'I know how much you used to love it, but of course you couldn't always afford it in the old days, could you? You're a lucky girl, dear,' she directed towards Abby again. 'I dare say there's nothing Ethan can't afford nowadays. You'll be living in clover.'

'I really hadn't thought about our future lifestyle,' Abby said stiffly.

'Really?' Vanessa laughed—a soft, sardonic sound.

They all ended up having cognac, Abby swallowing hers with an angry swiftness. It burned a path down her throat and into her brain, sparking fiery rebellion into her system. She would have liked to tell the bitch where to go, but she knew that Ethan would be furious with her if she made a scene in public. Still, when Vanessa suggested a second round, Abby decided that she'd had enough.

'I don't think so,' she said sharply. 'I'm quite tired after our long drive down. I'd like to go to bed now, darling, if you don't mind?' And she sent a glaring glance over her shoulder up at Ethan.

His returning gaze was cool. 'No, of course not, darling. Besides, too much alcohol has a tendency to deaden the system—especially at bedtime. Can't have that, can we?' he drawled rather icily. 'Well, goodnight, Vanessa. No doubt we'll have the opportunity to chat about old times some more over the coming weekend.'

So saying, he took Abby's hand, his grasp tightening as he led her from the room.

'I thought I told you to take my lead,' he bit out on the way down the stairs. 'In future, *I* will decide when we go to bed. I'm the boss, remember?'

By the time they reached the privacy of their room, she felt totally flustered and infuriated. She was suddenly very tired of playing this game, especially when she didn't know the rules.

She slammed the door behind her, glaring at Ethan's back as he strode over to open the mini-bar and pour himself a brandy. Abby only had to take one look at his body language to tell that nothing had changed between them. That kiss had meant nothing to him. *She* meant nothing to him. Nothing.

God, but it hurt, and the hurt was spurring her to say something. *Anything*!

'Deadening your system, Ethan?' she taunted.

He lanced her with a savage look. 'Just shut up, Abigail, *darling*. I've had quite enough for tonight.'

'And I've had *more* than enough!' she flung back at him, ripping off her earrings. 'What in hell did you think you were doing, saying we were engaged, then kissing me like that? That wasn't part of our deal.'

'Really? I would have thought the role of a fiancée much preferable for your reputation to being considered a mere lover, so what are you complaining about? Besides, you enjoyed that last kiss almost as much as I did. So is it more money that you want? Or more kisses? Or both?'

That did it. That really did it.

'Now, you listen here, you patronising, hypocritical prig! I won't even stoop to denying that I enjoyed your kiss, because yes, I did! I happen to be a normal woman, who likes good kissing on the whole, so don't take any satisfaction from that. But I *am* going to deny your ongoing implication that I'm some kind of hard-nosed mercenary piece who can be bought and sold for the right price.

'I demanded the particular fee I did because a sweet old lady I know was burgled last weekend, with all her savings stolen. Just over three thousand dollars. She was going to buy a second-hand electric wheelchair with that money and I simply couldn't bear to see her heartbreak, so I rang you up—which I'd vowed I wouldn't, believe me—and accepted your peculiar and quite pathetic proposal.

'I'm prepared to honour my word and see this through to the bitter end, but I will not be sneered at and put down and used without so much as a by-your-leave. Do I make myself clear?'

He stared at her, long and hard. 'Are you telling me the truth? About that old lady?'

'Of course I'm telling you the truth! Why would I lie?'

All the breath rushed out of his lungs, his shoulders sagging. All of a sudden he looked so tired—tired and grim and almost bewildered, as though everything which had sustained him for so long no longer existed.

God, but her heart went out to him. Her foolish female heart.

She came up to him, touched him on the arm. He turned and she looked into his bleak blue eyes, aching to make things better for him, to soothe him. 'Oh, Ethan,' she cried softly. 'Let it go. Let *her* go.'

His shoulders immediately straightened, his eyes hardening as he glared down at her. 'You don't know what you're talking about, woman. Now, let *me* go.' He shrugged her hand off his arm and she staggered backwards, more hurt than she could ever have thought possible.

'God, don't look at me like that,' he ground out, his glare changing to a frustrated frown. 'All right, so I misjudged you and I'm sorry. I'm sorry about a whole lot of things. But this still isn't any of your business, Abigail, so just keep out of it. Now, go to bed and leave me be. You can use the bed. I'll sleep on the sofa when I'm good and ready.'

CHAPTER ELEVEN

THEY were late for breakfast; Ann and Henry were just leaving the dining room as they were entering.

'You look like you didn't get much sleep last night, old chap,' Henry teased Ethan. 'I could go overseas with those bags you're sporting under your eyes.'

Abby wouldn't have been quite so blunt, but Henry was right. Ethan looked as if he'd been out on the tiles all night.

She had no idea what time he'd eventually turned in, but he'd still been nursing a drink at midnight, sitting silently in an armchair in the dark. When Abby had woken this morning, after a rather restless sleep herself, he'd been sprawled on the sofa asleep, still in his clothes, having not even bothered to pull out the bed.

Oddly, the dark rings under his eyes were not unattractive on him. Ethan was one of those men on whom the dissipated ravaged look was irritatingly attractive— something she'd noticed more than once over the last six months.

'You know what it's like, Henry,' Ethan returned offhandedly. 'Strange beds and all that.'

Henry chuckled drily. 'Sure, sure. That's your story and you're going to stick to it. You'd better get yourself into breakfast or you'll be late for the first lecture.'

'How about a game of tennis this morning, Abby?' Ann asked. 'Henry's challenged me to a match after lunch, and I need to get into practice.'

'Love to,' she answered. She needed to work off the calories that last night's dinner had already landed on her waistline. At the same time she might also work off some of the frustration she was feeling.

Ethan had showered and dressed in a brooding silence this morning, then snapped at her as they'd left the room that he hoped he could rely upon her to do what she'd been paid to do in future, and nothing more.

Abby had approached the dining room, and the day ahead, in a state of total confusion. Sylvia's pleas kept going round and round in her head. But, as she'd found out last night, it was impossible to keep Ethan away from Vanessa if he didn't want to be kept away.

'Meet me down at the tennis-courts at ten,' Ann called over her shoulder as she moved off down the stairs after a disappearing Henry.

'Will do,' Abby called back, then hurried after Ethan, who had already wandered into the dining room and was browsing along the breakfast buffet, plate in hand. Abby had just picked up her plate, and was trying to find something unfattening from the wide selection of food, when a murmuring sound made her glance round.

Vanessa had just swanned into the room on the arm of her puffy-faced, bleary-eyed husband, and was causing a stir of comments from those already seated.

There was plenty to comment on, Abby thought tartly—the woman's choice of a loose, shiny mauve trouser suit so resembling pyjamas that she looked as if she'd come to breakfast straight from bed. Her blonde hair had that tousled look which was incredibly sexy, and when she moved those too perfect, too firm, impossibly high breasts undulated under the silk, peaked nipples betraying their bra-less state.

Abby could hardly fail to notice that Ethan had also glanced around, and that his eyes were riveted to her just like all the other men's. She tried not to feel jealous, or worried, or even curious any more. But she failed miserably.

'She might be married to a neurosurgeon,' Abby muttered, 'but she's visited a few plastic surgeons in her day.'

Ethan slid her a drily amused look. 'Something *you* will certainly never need, my lovely Abigail, so don't be such a cat.'

Abby was startled by his compliment, till cynicism took over. 'And I thought you said you weren't a flatterer.'

'I'm not. You have the perfect female figure, and you know it.'

Abby flushed with both pleasure and surprise. She didn't know it all—her figure was far from perfect, she believed—but it thrilled her to think that Ethan thought it was.

Their eyes locked momentarily, and for the first time she was sure that she saw real desire lurking in those normally cool blue depths. It shook her. Maybe she'd been wrong last night about those kisses meaning nothing to him. Maybe he'd been as stirred by them as she had been.

'Don't just stand there, staring at me like that,' he snapped. 'You know damned well I've always found you a desirable woman. What normal man wouldn't? Now, hurry up and select some breakfast. Time is a-wasting.'

Abby was totally thrown by these new developments. He'd *always* desired her? It was an unsettling thought, and incredibly distracting. She found herself dithering terribly over what to eat, and in the end settled for orange juice, toast and coffee.

When they settled down at a table—unfortunately not far enough away from the table Vanessa and her husband were occupying—her nerves were so stretched that she was unable to eat more than a few mouthfuls. Aside from the shock of Ethan's announcement, she didn't like the way the blonde bombshell had looked her over as she'd carried her tray to the table—those big blue eyes scoffingly dismissive as they swept over her clothes.

Underneath, Abby knew that her designer jeans and simple striped bodysuit were quite suitable for the occasion, but Vanessa's scornful regard still irked her.

'You're not eating much,' Ethan commented as he tucked into his plate of bacon and eggs, belying Abby's earlier assumption that he'd had a distressing night and was in a mood. Surely a man in a mood—or pining over his lost love—would not have such a good appetite.

'I'm not hungry.'

He put down his knife and fork and just looked at her. 'Are you angry with me for snapping at you, or for finding you desirable?'

When she declined to answer that, he shrugged. 'Look, I realise I've been a bit of a pig. I wish I could explain...'

'Why can't you?'

He stared at her again, then shook his head. 'I can't risk it.'

'Risk what?'

'My sanity.'

'I don't understand, Ethan.'

'Better you don't, I think,' he said darkly.

'Tell me one thing. Are you still in love with Vanessa Ballistrat?'

His gaze slid over to the blonde, then back at Abby. 'You *have* to be joking,' he said, but far too vehemently.

Hate was the other side of love, wasn't it? Or was he admitting to a strictly sexual obsession?

'Then what is it with you and her? What game are you playing, Ethan?'

'A game as old as time, my sweet.'

'And what game is that?'

'Drink your coffee, Abigail. And stop worrying about what doesn't concern you.'

'But it *does* concern me, Ethan.'

'Why? It has nothing to do with you.'

'But it does, don't you see? You've involved me in this far more than you said you would. For one thing, Henry and Ann think we're genuinely engaged. Have you thought what you're going to tell Sylvia once they relay the news to her? And they will. Ann is an inveterate gossip.'

Ethan frowned. 'I hadn't thought of that.'

'I think there's a lot of things you haven't thought of, Ethan.'

He glared at her, and she would have loved to know what he was thinking. His glare slowly became a troubled frown. 'Yes,' he said slowly. 'Yes, I'm beginning to see that . . .'

'You . . . you're not going to do anything violent, are you, Ethan?'

'To whom?'

A strangely sexual glitter came into his ruthless blue eyes and she shivered. For he was looking at *her* at that moment.

'To . . . to Vanessa, of course,' she said shakily. 'Or to her husband.'

'Now, why would I do that?'

'I'm no fool, Ethan. I can read between the lines. You were lovers once, weren't you? And she jilted you when she ran off with Ballistrat.'

His face stiffened at her statement of the facts. His eyes grew tormented and her heart turned over at his obvious distress.

'Forget her, Ethan,' she urged. 'She's not worth it.'

His gaze slid slowly over to the woman who obviously still obsessed him, then back again. 'It's not that simple,' he said coldly.

'It *can* be.'

'No,' he denied. 'It can't. Now, finish your breakfast, Abigail, then go and play your tennis.'

She wanted to scream at him not to be so stupid or so blind. There were so many women in this world worth loving, but Vanessa Ballistrat was not one of them. But she could see that Ethan's mind and heart were closed to love. He was an embittered man who had come here seeking some kind of vengeance for Vanessa's betrayal of his love.

It worried Abby that he might still fall foul of that love again, that this clever, wicked woman might somehow ensnare his heart almost against his will. Her beauty and her womanly wiles were incredible, Abby could see. Not many men would stand a chance against her, once she set her sights on them.

Breakfast ended in a tense silence, with Abby glad to leave Ethan and be alone for a while in her room. She sat down on the side of the bed, her head whirling and her stomach churning.

What on earth was she going to do? How was she going to persuade Ethan that revenge was a self-destructive course, and not one which would lead to any happiness? Worse, how was she going to defuse that woman's potential power? She could not bear to think of that woman ever touching Ethan again, let alone kissing him. Or, God forbid, making love with him.

Maybe she should do what Sylvia had suggested. Seduce Ethan herself!

She wanted to. Dear God, she wanted to so much it had become a constant ache in her body. But she was afraid—afraid of getting emotionally involved with the man. Already she was being drawn deeper and deeper into his problems, wanting to solve them, wanting to protect him.

For her own sake she had to pull back, to distance herself from the situation. It really was none of her business, as Ethan had said more than once. And it was all getting out of hand!

Tennis was the answer. And swimming. And any other activity which would keep her busy, and tired, and away from Ethan.

Abby jumped up and stripped off her jeans and top in favour of her tennis gear—a very feminine lemon pleated skirt and matching T-shirt top, both edged in white. White socks and joggers completed the outfit, and Abby wrapped her hair into a tight knot on top of her head.

A glance in the mirror reassured her that she looked fine, though she still felt big compared with the petite and truly perfect Vanessa. Suddenly she couldn't wait to get onto the court and blast off a few of the offending inches.

There were four tennis-courts, clay-based and surrounded by tall rows of pines cleverly positioned to form a natural windbreak. The adjoining kiosk was well supplied with spare rackets, as well as several plastic tables and chairs for relaxing, and a refrigerator stocked with coolly refreshing non-alcoholic drinks.

'That's enough for me,' Abby said after their third set. She'd easily lost the first two before finding her own form and walloping Ann in the third. 'I'm shockingly unfit,' she said as they both collapsed into chairs with an iced mineral water.

'You don't look unfit,' Ann replied with an admiring glance. 'You have a fantastic figure.'

It was exactly what Abby needed to hear. She knew from experience that women did not flatter other women. 'That's sweet of you to say so, Ann, but I really could do with losing a few pounds. Some of my skirts are beginning to be a little tight.'

'I wouldn't worry too much about that, if I were you. Men don't mind tight skirts. They don't mind women with a few extra pounds on them either. Certainly not when they're as well distributed as yours.'

Ann leant forward suddenly, dropping her voice a little. 'Tell me to mind my own business if you want to, but did Ethan and Vanessa Ballistrat have something going once?'

'Perhaps. Perhaps not,' Abby returned, battling hard to keep her voice casual. 'Frankly, I don't really care if he did. I don't believe in a woman cross-questioning a man about his past love-life. The past is the past.'

'I agree, but it's foolish to put your head in the sand where a woman like that is concerned. I'd watch her, if I were you. I think she's after Ethan.'

Abby could not help the stricken look which crossed her face.

'Oh, dear. Perhaps I shouldn't have said anything. It's just that it's perfectly obvious you absolutely adore

Ethan. The way you looked at him last night after he kissed you...'

Abby opened her mouth then shut it again, simply unable to speak at that moment.

'Men can be such fools sometimes,' Ann went on. 'And females like that Venus fly-trap can be so unscrupulous. If Dr Ballistrat is having money troubles, she won't stay with him. That's the way women like that work. If she and Ethan have already been lovers, and if she senses he still feels anything for her at all, it's only natural he'd be the one she might try to trap next. And, let's face it, she's got a lot of equipment for setting traps...'

Abby felt quite ill. Not because of the warning about Vanessa. She had already conceded the possibility of Ethan falling back into her clutches. No, Abby's distress came from Ann's words—'it's perfectly obvious you absolutely adore Ethan.'

I do, she realised, her head spinning. I adore him. And I want him like mad. Oh, God, I must love him. I thought I couldn't possibly, simply because I didn't like him, but my foolish female heart simply bypassed liking and went straight to love.

'Oh, my dear, please don't look like that,' Ann pleaded. 'I didn't mean to worry you. I'm terribly sorry. Please forget what I said. No sane man could prefer that woman to you.'

No sane man...

The words echoed in Abby's brain.

But Ethan wasn't sane where that woman was concerned. She'd festered in his brain for years, distorting his view of women, making him suffer a coldly cynical existence rather than trust another woman with his heart. Sylvia had recognised his madness. That was why she'd been so worried about his coming here, why she'd begged Abby to keep him away from Vanessa.

'Excuse me, but can either of you two ladies help us out? We'd like to play a set of doubles but there's only three of us.'

Abby looked up at the three eager-faced ladies and shook her head. 'I couldn't,' she murmured, still feeling shattered. 'You play, Ann.'

Ann groaned.

'Please,' the three women chorused.

'Oh, all right,' Ann sighed. 'But only one set.'

She left and Abby was alone. With a moan she put her elbows on the table and sank her head into her hands, her eyes closing.

How could I have allowed this to happen? Didn't Dillon teach me anything? God, am I going to spend the rest of my life falling in love with the wrong men?

I'll really have to quit working for him now, she accepted bleakly. I refuse to go on being some kind of martyr to my silly feelings. Hell, I despise women who love men who don't love them back. How self-destructive can you get?

'Have a headache, do we?'

Abby whipped her hands away just as Vanessa pulled out the chair Ann had not long vacated. The mauve silk outfit suggested that she hadn't come down to play tennis.

'No, no headache,' Abby returned coolly. 'Just tired. I've been playing tennis.'

'So I noticed earlier on. I was taking a stroll around the gardens. When I saw your friend returning for another game I came round in search of the missing Miss Richmond.'

'Really? Why?' Abby snapped.

'There's no need to be rude.'

'I think there's every reason to be rude.' Abby was not going to pull any punches. She'd found in prison that when dealing with people like Vanessa politeness was interpreted as weakness, and tact as stupidity. 'I don't like you any more than you like me. I also know what you're up to, so don't feed me any of your manipulative lies. Say what you have to say, then get the hell out of my sight.'

'My, my, not so much the polite little lady after all, are we?'

'No, so don't you forget it.'

'Meaning what?'

'Meaning you come round batting your false eyelashes at Ethan any more, and I'll tear your equally false boobs off.'

She gasped and staggered not so gracefully to her feet. 'I'm going to tell Ethan you said that!'

'Go ahead. He'll laugh himself silly.'

Those blue eyes narrowed nastily as she quickly gathered herself. 'You don't know who you're dealing with.'

'I know exactly *what* I'm dealing with. An amoral, mercenary bitch.'

'You're going to be sorry you said that.'

'I doubt it.'

Abby was lashed by a look that would have shrivelled a lesser woman. She looked boldly back at her adversary and had the satisfaction of Vanessa being the first to look away and stalk off.

'You won't win,' Abby muttered under her breath. 'I don't care what I have to do. The man I love is not going to end up in your clutches again. No, siree!'

CHAPTER TWELVE

'I'M GOING back to my room,' Abby shouted out across the tennis-court, and Ann waved her approval.

Fifteen minutes later Abby was standing in the bathroom, biting her bottom lip as she grimaced at her reflection in the mirror. She had been staring at herself in horror for some time.

The black bikini was more outrageous than ever. She seemed to be spilling out everywhere. No matter how she tried to spread the gathered cups which inadequately encased her C-cup breasts, they always concertinaed back down into two narrow strips of material which only just covered her nipples.

The bottom half was just as bad—two skimpy triangles, joined at the sides with the flimsiest ties, and legs so high-cut that she'd almost had to shave herself bare to be presentable. God knows what the back view was like!

Sighing, she opened the bathroom door and backed up a bit, standing on tiptoe to get a longer view of her hips and legs in the waist-high vanity mirror. Gritting her teeth, she half turned and glanced over her shoulders at her behind. Dear heavens, the amount of creamy flesh on display was appalling.

'I could never wear this in public,' she muttered dispiritedly. And there she'd been thinking she could out-seduce Vanessa by prancing around the pool in front of Ethan in this.

'I agree.'

Abby squawked, whirling as her eyes darted around the room, her heart pounding. Ethan was lounging back in the armchair nearest the window, his arms outstretched, his ankles crossed. The sunlight was behind him, which cast his face into shadow, so she couldn't see either his features or his expression.

She went quite hot all over, at the same time wishing there was something at hand she could snatch up and cover herself with. 'I...I didn't hear you come in,' she stammered. 'And what do you mean, you agree?' she snapped, almost as an afterthought. 'I think I look pretty good!' Abby was never at her best when someone tried to put her down these days.

'You know damned well you don't look pretty good,' Ethan drawled. 'You look bloody fantastic.'

'Oh...'

Ethan rose slowly to his feet, his considerable height blocking out a good proportion of the light. 'But you're right about wearing it in public,' he said ruefully. 'I think you should keep it for my eyes only.'

Abby blinked, the atmosphere in the room suddenly charged with an electric sexual tension. She knew now, without seeing his eyes, that they were staring at her body, and not with disgust but with desire. It sent a thrill racing all through her—a dangerously exciting thrill. Her face flamed and her body followed suit.

When he started walking towards her she remained exactly where she was, her chin tipped almost defiantly upwards while her mind recklessly willed him on. Her heart began to hammer against her ribs as he drew nearer, but when his eyes came into view there was nothing of desire in them, only a coolly speculative regard.

Abby was utterly thrown.

'What... what are you doing here?' she asked shakily when he stopped just in front of her. 'You should still be in conference for another half-hour.'

'I had a headache,' he explained, his eyes dropping to her breasts, which were rising and falling with betraying speed. 'I needed something for it.'

'Oh...'

'It's gone now,' he said, and quite calmly, even coldly, reached around behind her and untied her bra top, tossing it nonchalantly away.

Abby didn't say a word, merely stared at him in shock as a horrified elation raced through her. He bent and brushed his lips over hers while he played with her breasts, his hands gentle, yet oddly merciless. She sensed that they would not stop if she asked. *He* would not stop.

But she didn't want him to stop, did she? She loved the man and wanted him like crazy. Besides, this was the perfect way to defuse any sexual power Vanessa might hold over him.

Ethan was as she'd always suspected as a lover. Ruthless, and cold, and, yes, machine-like. Yet for all that... incredibly exciting. There was no hint of seduction in his movements, however, merely a steely resolve. No hint of making love to her, merely cold-blooded caresses designed to arouse her sufficiently to suit his dark purpose.

Perversely, Abby found that a real turn-on. It was so different from Dillon, who had dressed everything up with flowery words and false promises. How many times had Dillon said he loved her while he made love to her?

Lies. All lies.

There would be none of that from Ethan. He was only offering her sex, and even though she loved him, and might secretly hope for more, she admired his unspoken honesty. Oh, yes, she could cope with this type of love-making far better than Dillon's lies.

Cope? Oh, God...what an inadequate word for the feelings rampaging through her. She was already dizzy with desire, aching and yearning for more.

When his hands abandoned her throbbing breasts she groaned her disappointment, only to gasp when they slid smoothly down her sides to untie the ineffective bows on her hips. Simultaneously his mouth deepened his kiss, perhaps to keep her distracted while he stripped the scrap of material away.

Abby was beyond caring what his motives were, as long as he kept his mouth on hers and his hands on her flesh. She moaned softly under the relentless rhythm of his tongue, then moaned anew when one of his hands slipped between her thighs to set up another, far more relentless rhythm.

She could hardly believe the sensations, or the wanting. Her body strained against his knowing touch. She tensed. Then trembled.

He took her so close, so terrifyingly close, before he stopped and lay her throbbing, burning body back across the bed, coolly watching her mindless arousal drain away while he undressed with meticulous measured movements, placing each item of clothing neatly on a nearby chair.

Abby's heartbeat finally regained some normality, her brain and body galvanised by his cold control. Even when he was naked, with his stark erection flaunting his need, he seemed totally composed, joining her on the bed and setting about re-arousing her with a second session of calculating kisses and caresses till she was once again balancing on that razor's edge.

'Please don't stop,' she begged breathlessly. 'Oh, God...'

Only then did he spread her legs wide and move between them, bending her knees back to angle her body to fit perfectly to his.

Abby squeezed her eyes shut in anticipation of Ethan's body invading her, but when it came her eyes flung back open, so stunned was she by the feel of his flesh as it probed, then pushed inside her. He was much the same size as Dillon. Yet he felt so different.

It had to be *her* who was different, she finally realised. She was far more turned on than she'd ever been with Dillon, her body enclosing Ethan's with a greedy, grasping need which would never let him go till it had milked him dry.

Her head spun as he slid deeper and deeper inside her, and she moaned her ecstasy.

His penetration finally complete, he wrapped her legs high around his back then began surging into her, his body as relentless as his tongue and his hands had been.

He was inhuman, she thought despairingly, his face a mask of perfect concentration as he pumped robotically into her, not a flicker of emotion to disturb the symmetry of his classically handsome features. Yet *she* was swiftly beside herself, her head threshing from side to side, her hands clenching and unclenching as she tried to prolong the pleasure and stop herself coming.

The thought of him coldly watching her face convulse in the throes of a climax was suddenly anathema to her. She wanted him to come with her. She wanted him wild and unthinking, his own face all twisted with a raw, primitive ecstasy which he could only ever find with her. She could not bear his machine-like performance another moment. There was a living, breathing, passionate man somewhere beneath that cold, calculating façade, and she meant to find him.

Her actions were instinctive—her hands reaching up to run feverishly over his stiffly held shoulders, then up his corded neck towards his suddenly taut face muscles. His mouth gasped open when she began to trace his lips boldly with her fingers. She didn't hesitate, daringly inserting them into his mouth, sliding them back and forth along his wet tongue in an echo of what his body was doing inside hers.

'Ethan,' she moaned in her mad passion for him. 'Oh, Ethan...'

He froze for a second, then shuddered violently, a raw, animal sound punched from his lungs. He began sucking ravenously on her fingers and pounding her body in a mad frenzy of desire. Abby's already sensitised flesh immediately responded, and she rocketed to a climax with him, her fingers falling from his mouth when his back arched violently away from her. Her own mouth fell open and she gasped breath after ragged breath into her starving lungs.

Ethan swore, then collapsed onto the bed beside her, taking her with him so that she was lying sprawled across his chest. His hands felt furious as they cupped her face and lifted it from his still heaving chest, forcing her to look down at him and witness his torment.

'Why in hell did you do that?' he growled, gasping for breath between outbursts. 'I meant to protect us...or at least pull out... You shouldn't have done that... You should have stopped me... Hell, why didn't you?'

Stop him? Was he joking? She couldn't have stopped him even if she'd wanted to.

Abby expelled a long, quivering sigh. The heat of the moment was quickly giving way to a rotten reality. Still,

Abby had long since become a realist. She'd known what she was doing when she allowed Ethan to make love to her, known what to expect from him afterwards.

Nothing.

But it still hurt. God, when would she ever learn? 'It's all right, Ethan,' she managed in a relatively calm voice. 'If you're worried about my getting pregnant, then don't be. If you're worried about anything else, then don't be as well. I've never had unprotected sex before. I hope you can give me the same assurance.'

'Don't be ridiculous,' he said, staring at her as though she were mad. 'Of course I can.'

Abby almost laughed. She should have guessed that this was the first time Ethan had lost his much vaunted control and done something really rash. A type of triumph softened any hurt at his presumption that any risk would come from her.

'Are you absolutely *sure* you won't get pregnant?' he demanded hoarsely.

Abby didn't really want to discuss the issue. She'd always believed that a pregnancy which resulted from an act of love was not something which could be wiped away with a pill or an operation. And it *had* been an act of love. For her.

In truth, the risk was minimal this weekend, and would grow less with every passing day. She knew her body well and should have ovulated earlier in the week. Nine times out of ten, she would have. There were times, though, when her cycle could surprise her—usually when she was under stress.

She thought of all that had happened last weekend and made a silent prayer.

'There is no risk,' she said aloud. 'My period's due soon, and I'm disgustingly regular.'

'I can write you a prescription for a morning-after pill, if you'd like.'

'Oh, do shut up, Ethan. You're spoiling the moment.'

He stared at her. 'What moment?'

'You and me, abandoning our mutual hostility.'

He almost choked on the spot, then gave a harsh bark of laughter. 'I should have known sex with you would not be like sex with any other woman. Hell, it certainly wasn't. I've never known anything like it.'

'Should I be flattered by that remark?'

'No, complimented. As I said before, I don't believe in flattery. You're damned good in bed, you know that?'

'I'm not in bed. I'm on top of you.'

'Which is another perspective we must explore in the near future,' he said darkly.

'How near?'

Abby tried to feel shock at her eager voice but could not. Already she was addicted to his mouth, his touch, his body. It had never been like this for her before. With Dillon she hadn't always reached a climax, and when she had it had always taken ages. It had been less than ten minutes since Ethan had taken her bra off.

Already, she wanted him again. Ten minutes wasn't nearly enough. She wanted a whole lifetime of his love-making, dammit. But, failing that, she would take whatever she could get as often as she could get it. Keeping him away from Vanessa would be an added bonus.

'How about after lunch?' he suggested, rubbing one of his thumbs backwards and forwards across her puffy lips.

Her heart leapt even as she frowned. 'We're supposed to be playing tennis with Ann and Henry.'

'Leave it to me,' he said, before pulling her harshly down onto his mouth and swiftly showing her that she would always be at his mercy. Always.

It was a telling and troubling thought, and one Abby promised herself that she would address when this weekend was over. Meanwhile she had neither the strength nor the will to resist him. He could command, and demand, and she knew that she would simply say yes.

Yes. Yes. Yes.

'Do you like making love in the afternoon?' he muttered thickly against her bruised mouth.

'Mmm,' was all she could manage. He'd idly begun to massage the small of her back and her buttocks, and it was sending her thoughts into a spin.

'And in the middle of the night?'

She made a small moan of assent. Dear God, he was actually swelling inside her again, filling her own still sensitised flesh for the second mind-blowing time within fifteen minutes. She hadn't known a man could do that. Dillon never had.

'And in the morning?'

'Yes,' she gasped.

'What about just before lunch?' He pushed her upright on him, gripping her hips and ruthlessly urging her to ride him.

'Yes,' she choked out, just before she closed her eyes and lost all control. Again.

CHAPTER THIRTEEN

ABBY poured herself another glass of wine, took a sip, then turned to walk over and peek through the drawn curtains at the setting sun.

'Pull the curtain back. I want a better look at you.'

She did as Ethan asked before glancing over her shoulder at him.

He was lying on the rumpled bed, a sheet dragged across his lower half, his head and shoulders propped up against a mountain of pillows. He was sipping a Scotch. He was also staring at her, his hard blue eyes glittering with a decidedly primitive desire.

Abby could not believe how quickly Ethan had stripped her of all inhibition where her body was concerned. She'd never been this comfortable before, walking around naked. Now she not only did so without shyness, she found the experience a turn-on.

What an incredible afternoon, she thought as she gazed at Ethan.

He'd made love to her swiftly and urgently on their return to the room after lunch, taking her up against the door, leaving her unsatisfied and wildly excited. Afterwards, he'd undressed them both and carried her into the shower, where he'd washed her in a most erotic fashion, keeping her aroused at the same time.

'No,' he'd ordered when she'd automatically reached for a robe afterwards. 'I want you naked. And your hair down.'

Which was exactly how she'd spent the rest of the afternoon. Naked, with her hair down, and totally at his sexual disposal.

He'd finally let her come... after a long hour of exquisite torment, stunning her then by giving her climax after climax in quick succession. She was powerless against his expertise, especially that merciless mouth of his. He'd taken his time in using that last weapon against her. But when he had, he'd driven her mad.

She'd made love to him with her mouth in return—something Dillon had surprisingly never pressed for, but which she'd always been sure she would hate.

But she hadn't hated it at all. She'd felt a heady sense of power as she'd driven Ethan once again to lose control. When she'd stopped momentarily, to push her hair out of her eyes, he'd actually begged her to go on. God, but she'd revelled in his guttural pleas, exulted wildly in his mindless surrender to her ministrations. She couldn't wait to do it again.

'Henry didn't believe your migraine story for a moment, you know,' she said. This was their first real conversation all afternoon.

'Neither your excuse that you were tired and wanted to read,' he returned drily.

'No.'

'Has it occurred to you that what you told Henry and Ann about us has partly come true?'

Abby frowned. 'What did I say to them?'

'About our pent-up feelings exploding. I can't speak for you, but I know it was true in my case. I've been wanting to do this from the first moment I laid eyes on you.'

Abby was startled. 'Really?'

Now *he* was startled. 'You mean you didn't know? I thought you saw it in my eyes the very first time I looked at you. You looked shocked at *something*.'

'I was surprised how young you were. And how handsome.'

'I wasn't at all surprised how good-looking *you* were,' he said drily. 'I had a feeling Sylvia would line up some delectable young thing to tempt me.'

Abby had to smile. 'And did I tempt you?'

His own smile was rueful. 'Excruciatingly so. I used to dread Fridays, yet I enjoyed them too, in a perverse way. You've no idea the thoughts that used to go through my head. It was all I could manage to keep a straight face.' He took another sip of his drink, his eyes turning speculative. 'So how *have* you felt about me all this while?'

'I hated you,' she confessed, despite seeing now that that hate had been the other side of love.

He laughed. But it was a bitter sound. 'Then don't stop, for God's sake. There's no future with me, Abigail. I'm poison to any woman. Frankly, I just can't bring myself to trust women, especially beautiful ones. I probably never will.'

She stared at his coldly bitter eyes, and knew that he was telling the truth. There would never be any future with him. Not a real one. She'd been silly to begin hoping for it.

'Don't worry,' she said. 'I won't go falling in love with you any time in the future.' Can't, she thought with wry irony, I've already done that.

'I didn't think you would. You and I are alike, my sweet. You've been hurt too. And you're tough. I like that. Of course, I don't want you hating my making love to you. I have plans for you where that's concerned.'

'Are you saying you want us to remain lovers when we go back to Sydney?'

'Yes, of course.'

Abby's heart contracted. 'What about my job on Fridays?'

'I didn't lie to Henry. I'm going to send Sylvia on an extended holiday. She deserves it. Work for me full-time as well. I see you're a girl with pride and that you wouldn't want me setting you up as some kind of kept woman. I'll pay you a good salary and I'll treat you well. I promise.'

Abby swallowed. He was dressing it up to sound respectable, but she knew exactly what he was asking. On the surface she might be his receptionist, but underneath...underneath, she would still be his mistress. He was trying to buy her body as surely as he might buy the lowest streetwalker. She wasn't sure if she could do that to herself. Yet she wasn't sure if she had the strength to say no.

'We'll see, Ethan,' was all she said for the moment, and took another sip of her drink, watching him closely over the rim of her glass. He wasn't a man to take a refusal lightly, even the possibility of one.

His eyes narrowed with ruthless resolve upon her. 'Come here.'

An unbidden quiver of excitement rippled down her spine and she obeyed, though not at any speed, her walk slow and seductive across the room. 'What do you want?' she asked as she stood beside the bed.

He reached up, curled his hand around a long lock of her hair and pulled her down onto the bed, the abrupt action sending her wine spilling all over his chest. 'You know what I want,' he grated out.

'Say it, then,' she whispered harshly, suddenly wanting some kind of revenge for his ruthless using of her. 'Say it,' she ordered him.

He said it.

She threw back the sheet and bent her mouth to where the wine had spilled over his chest. She licked up the droplets with calculating slowness, lingering over his male nipples for an excruciatingly long time before working her way ever so slowly downwards.

He was groaning long before she reached her ultimate target.

'Wear this tonight,' Ethan ordered, pulling the coffee-coloured lace dress out of the wardrobe and tossing it across her still naked body.

'Say please,' she purred.

'Please.'

She laughed. 'You're the only man I've ever known who could make the word "please" sound like an order as well.'

He grabbed her wrist as she slid off the bed, and pulled her to him, only the dress between their naked bodies. 'And how many men *have* you known, darling heart? Biblically speaking.'

His sudden black jealousy startled her.

She searched his eyes for what lay behind it, hoping and praying but not at all confident. 'Would you believe me if I said only one before you?'

Clearly it was a struggle for him to do so.

'Never mind,' she said drily. 'It doesn't matter, does it?'

His face filled with torment. 'It shouldn't—but, damn it all, it does!'

'Then *believe* me, Ethan,' she urged with a quiet desperation. 'Believe me.'

'I want to.'

'What's stopping you?'

'It just doesn't make sense. You're so beautiful and desirable. I can't stop wanting you. Many other men must have wanted you just as much,' he groaned, and bent to kiss her.

His dark passion sparked an equally dark passion within herself. She let the dress fall to the floor between them and slid her arms up around his neck, Ethan sucking in a sharp breath as she rubbed the still hardened tips of her breasts against his bare chest.

'And you're far too good at this,' he rasped against her mouth.

'In that case just shut up and enjoy, Ethan. I haven't asked you how many lovers you've had, have I?'

'No, but that's because you don't—' He broke off, his mouth twisting into an agonised grimace.

'Don't what?' she whispered, dying for him to kiss her again, to touch her. Why did he have to ask stupid questions at times like this?

'Never mind,' he growled, and, grabbing her by the waist, he picked her up and tossed her back onto the bed.

'You're a wonderful dancer,' Ethan praised in a husky whisper, his breath warm against her ear.

They'd dined with Henry and Ann earlier in the evening, then the four of them had come down to where there was dancing in the ballroom.

Abby took Ethan's compliment as the truth. There hadn't been much call for dancing in prison, although the girls had sometimes put the radio on and mucked around. But, hell, nine years of ballet, tap and modern had to count for something!

'You're a pretty good dancer yourself,' she said, thinking that it was as well she could execute the right steps without thinking. Concentration was impossible with her body moulded to Ethan's from chest to thigh.

'And you smell delicious,' he murmured. 'What's that perfume you've been wearing this weekend?'

'Chanel No. 5.'

'Another gift, I suppose. Women don't buy perfume like that for themselves. Now don't get huffy,' he went on swiftly when she stiffened under his taunt, 'I seem to have developed an irrational case of jealousy where you're concerned. I can only apologise for my own hypocrisy in expecting you not to have a past. Damn it all, mine's not too wonderful.'

Ethan's mention of a past made her think of her stay in prison for the first time this weekend. She wished that she could tell him about it, but knew that to do so would be a disaster.

'I picked the right dress for dancing, didn't I?' he chuckled, the hand in the small of her back exerting some more inward pressure as he whirled her round.

He was referring to her braless state, of course, as well as the figure-hugging nature of the gown. Abby had given in to his request to wear the dress, despite knowing that it would be extra tight and that the off-the-shoulder and daringly low neckline would mean she'd be half-naked underneath it. It had taken her ages to do up the back zipper, and a lot of breathing in.

Now the dress felt like a corset over her curves, the cool silk lining making her hotly aware of her erect nipples, especially when Ethan pressed her hard against him, as he was doing at this moment. Thank God the

skirt flared out from the hips or she would not have
been able to move, let alone dance.

'You're wicked, do you know that?' she whispered
shakily.

'Then we're a good pair, aren't we?' he countered in
a low, thickened voice. 'Do shut up, Abby. I want to
savour the moment, not chat about it.'

Abby felt a momentary jab of dismay that she hadn't
really managed to change his opinion about her. Of
course, she had only herself to blame. She should never
have invented that sugar-daddy lover. Once again, it
crossed her mind to tell him the whole truth. But would
he believe her?

She doubted it. All she would probably achieve was
a cessation of their relationship, such as it was, plus the
loss of her job. No, she wasn't about to risk either of
those things. She loved Ethan too much to lose what
little of him she had. Her desire to protect herself from
future hurt was simply not as strong as her desire for
the man. It was as simple as that.

So Abby closed her eyes, buried her face into his neck
and savoured as well, revelling in the feel of his hard
body pressed up against her and the promise of pleasure
to come...when the dancing was over.

Ethan's muttered 'Good God' had her lifting her head
and looking up at him.

'What is it?'

'Nothing for you to worry about.'

Abby's natural curiosity still had her glancing around
the ballroom. She didn't have to look round for long.
Madame Vanessa had just made an entrance, dressed in
the most outrageous red satin gown Abby had ever seen.
Halter-necked, it had a V-neckline in front plunging to
her waist, which was cinched with a wide jewelled belt.

There was no back to speak of, and the skirt was so tight that she could not possibly be wearing a stitch underneath.

Once again, Philip Ballistrat was nowhere in sight, and his adultery-seeking wife was immediately claimed for a dance by a male admirer. She went into his arms as if she belonged there, a seductive smile on her full red lips.

'At least she's wearing the right colour for a scarlet woman,' Abby said tartly.

'True.'

Ethan's agreement sparked some hope in Abby that his ex-flame had shown her true colours to him at last, thereby laying her ghost to rest once and for all.

'You... you don't care about her any more, do you, Ethan? I mean... she might be beautiful and sexy, but she's very shallow and superficial, you know.'

'Yes, I know.'

'Know that she's beautiful and sexy? Or that she's shallow and superficial?'

'Both.'

Jealousy had her pulling out of his arms a fraction, but he pulled her right back. 'Don't be silly,' he growled. 'She's not nearly as beautiful and sexy as you.'

'What about shallow and superficial?' she challenged archly. 'I hope you don't think I'm just as shallow and superficial!'

'I wish I did. But I have a feeling there are depths to you, Abigail, my love, which I haven't even begun to discover yet.' His lips moved over her hair and she shivered. 'You're such an enigmatic creature,' he murmured. 'A chameleon. I don't know what to make of you sometimes. But, frankly, I'm not keen to discover those other depths just yet. I might not like them. I just want to enjoy you for now.' He kissed her hair and pressed her even closer.

Abby wanted to cry. For he'd just spelled it out for her, hadn't he? Even with Vanessa out of the way, he didn't want *her* for anything more than sexual pleasure. It was as cut and dried as that.

She gazed with shattered eyes over Ethan's shoulder, hoping to distract herself from her emotional state by looking around the elegant ballroom. Her eyes were travelling from couple to couple when the glimpse of a face across the crowded room had her grinding to a shocked halt.

'What's wrong?' Ethan asked, pulling back and glancing down at her with a puzzled frown.

'I...er...I...nothing. A slight dizzy spell.'

'You're as white as a sheet. Do you want to sit down?'

'What? Yes...er...yes, I think I might. But not here. I'll go to the restroom. Perhaps a glass of water will help. No, don't come with me. I'll be fine.'

'If you're sure. I'll talk to Henry and Ann while you're gone. Take your time.'

Abby fled to the ladies' and hid in the toilet cubicle for a while, afraid to go back to the ballroom lest she find out that she was right, and that that face actually belonged to whom she thought it did. She finally emerged from the cubicle, only to find that same face staring back at her in the powder-room mirror.

'Abby!' the woman exclaimed.

Abby's heart sank. Of all the rotten luck. 'Hello, Dr Seymour,' she said, struggling to keep her voice calm. 'What on earth are you doing here?'

'Having a well-earned rest. I'm not here professionally. Just as a wife. My husband's a surgeon.'

'Oh...'

'And you, Abby? What are you doing here?'

She took a deep breath and hoped she'd covered her shock well. Who would have believed that the prison psychiatrist and counsellor would turn up at a surgeons' conference? It hadn't remotely occurred to Abby that doctors tended to marry doctors.

'I'm here with my fiancé,' she said. 'He's a doctor.' The moment the words were out of her mouth she wished she hadn't said them. She should have said that she was just here with a friend.

'Oh, who? Would I know him?'

Abby swallowed. She'd done it now. 'Dr Grant. Dr Ethan Grant.'

'The orthopaedic surgeon?'

'Yes, that's right.'

'I don't know him personally, but I've heard of him. He's an excellent doctor—and very handsome, if I've heard correctly.'

'I've been working as his receptionist,' Abby offered, feeling a little better that Ethan and Dr Seymour's husband weren't colleagues in any way.

'But how wonderful! I'm so happy for you, my dear. I didn't think you'd be able to put that other awful business behind you too easily, but it seems you've managed splendidly. It just shows what true love can do. It can restore trust and make life worthwhile again, can't it?'

'Yes,' Abby said weakly.

'I hope you'll be very happy, my dear. I always believed in your total innocence and it seems someone else does too. That must make up for your family's attitude. Or has your father finally come round?'

'No,' Abby said stiffly. 'No, he hasn't come round.'

'That's too bad. And what about your mother?'

'Nothing's changed on that score either.'

Dr Seymour gave a sad sigh. 'Never mind. You can't force someone to believe you. You have the love of a good man now, which must be some consolation. Be totally honest with him and I'm sure you'll be fine. Promise me you'll do that?'

Tears welled up in Abby's eyes and she valiantly blinked them away. 'I'll try. I...I must go,' she added tautly. 'Ethan will be wondering where I am.'

'Of course. Look after yourself, dear. I'm so glad to see you again. I've often thought of you.'

Abby almost ran back to the ballroom, her thoughts and emotions a-jumble. If she'd been able to, she would have kept on running—away from Dr Seymour and the heartbreaking memories she evoked, away from Ethan and the new heartbreak he was going to create for her.

But she knew that she couldn't. She loved him, and wanted him, and her hungry eyes were searching for him the moment she returned to the crowded room.

Those eyes opened wide when she found him, shock and dismay mingling to clamp her heart into a painful vice. For he was dancing with that scarlet-clad bitch, his arms wrapped tightly around her, his eyes clamped to hers as they swirled around the polished floor, their bodies and legs perfectly attuned. Abby felt sick as she watched them, sensing in that moment that here was something Ethan would never feel for her.

For this had once been true love, despite its bitter ending—an obsessive love which had left Ethan a hard shell of a man who used silly women like herself to satisfy his carnal lusts while secretly yearning for the one woman who'd meant something to him.

She paled as she watched them together. They were oblivious to the other couples dancing around them, ob-

livious of their surroundings, oblivious of Abby watching
them with her heart bleeding and breaking into little
pieces. She saw both of Ethan's hands move caressingly
over Vanessa's bare back, saw her slender white arms
slide seductively around his neck, saw her tip her lovely
head under his chin.

She could watch no more, whirling and fleeing back
to her room, banging the door shut behind her and
throwing herself onto the bed before bursting into loud
noisy sobs. She was still weeping wretchedly when Ethan
walked in some time later.

'Why didn't you come back to the ballroom?' he demanded abruptly. 'And why are you crying?'

She dashed away her tears, rolled over and glared up
at him, using anger as a survival weapon. 'Because!'

'Because why?'

'Because you're a bastard and I hate you!'

He sighed. 'You saw me dancing with Vanessa.'

Abby laughed. '*Dancing?* I wouldn't call what you
two were doing dancing,' she sneered. 'You lied to me
about still caring for that bitch. You've been using me,
Ethan. Making love to *me* while you've been thinking
about *her*. And you humiliated me tonight. If you recall,
I'm supposed to be your fiancée. I hate and despise you.'

'We've already established that.'

'I won't ever be your lover again after this! Never ever.'

'Don't say that,' he groaned.

Abby stared at his suddenly bleak face and felt total
confusion. What was she going to do with this man?

'Believe me when I say what you saw meant nothing,'
he insisted fiercely. 'It was just something I had to do,
a test I had to make. You're not a fool, Abby. You were
right when you guessed there was something between
Vanessa and myself once. But we were more than just

lovers. We were engaged to be married. The wedding was only a fortnight away when she dumped me for Ballistrat. I thought I'd never gotten over her and what she did. Which is why I came down here. But I soon realised I had. Well and truly. Still, when she came up to me and asked me to dance with her, I thought it would be a good idea to make certain.'

'And?'

'And nothing. She's pathetic. More than pathetic. She's so rotten to the core, I can't believe I ever loved her.'

'But you did.'

'I thought I did. But I was also only twenty-five years old, and even back then she was very sophisticated in matters of men and sex. Maybe that explains it. It wasn't love. It was a sexual infatuation.'

'And you don't desire her any more?'

'I almost felt sick tonight, touching her.'

Funny. He hadn't looked sick when she saw him. But he always was good at putting on a façade.

'I'd much rather touch you,' he said, sitting down beside her on the bed and running a tantalising finger around the deep neckline of her dress.

'No, don't,' she protested weakly, despite her pulse-rate immediately taking off.

'Don't be silly. You want me to.' And he rolled her over and began slowly unzipping her dress.

'Oh, God,' she gasped when he bent his mouth to the nape of her neck. It moved inexorably down her bared spine as he peeled the dress back with his hands.

Abby was instantly breathless with desire, spellbound with a heart-pounding excitement.

Yes, kiss me there, she moaned silently. Then *not* so silently.

'Don't stop,' she gasped on one occasion. 'Please don't stop.'

He kept her face down while he stripped her, sensitising each square inch of her body as it became exposed to his mouth and his oh, so clever hands.

He did not stop the erotic torment. Not for a moment.

By the time he finally fused his flesh with hers she was writhing beneath him, grasping the quilt with clenched fists, her cheek hot against the pillow. Her only consolation was that he appeared as mindlessly impassioned as she was, blind to everything but her body and the pleasure he seemed to find there.

She cried out his name as she came. Then simply cried, her face buried and turned away from him. She tried to resist his taking her in his arms afterwards, but she was too exhausted to resist.

'Hush, my love,' he soothed, rocking her in his arms. 'Hush.'

But she cried till she fell asleep. For she knew that she was not his love. And never would be.

CHAPTER FOURTEEN

'I DIDN'T do it,' Abby cried aloud in her sleep. 'I didn't. You have to believe me. Oh, God, why don't you believe me?'

'Abby.' Ethan shook her by the shoulder. 'Abby wake up. You're having a nightmare.'

She sat bolt-upright in the bed, staring around her for a few confused seconds before she realised where she was, and that the real nightmare she'd once lived through was not actually happening all over again.

It was just a dream that came whenever she was upset. In it, she would be back in that courtroom, trying to convince everyone of the truth, but no one would believe her. No one.

The worst thing was that it always *seemed* so real!

'Oh, thank God,' she cried with a rush of relief.

When Ethan's arms went round her she shuddered, then with a strangled sob buried her face in his chest. 'It was just a dream,' she cried in muffled tones. 'Just a dream...'

He gathered her tightly to him and began stroking her hair back from her face. 'Just a dream, my love.'

Abby stiffened at the endearment and went to pull away, but he would have none of it, holding her even more tightly.

'Tell me about it,' he insisted.

She looked up into his shadowed face, unable to see the expression in his eyes, the only light in the room some faint moonlight coming through the window.

156

'I...I don't think so.' It was all very well for Dr Seymour to say be honest, but being honest didn't automatically mean being believed.

'Tell me, Abby,' he urged.

'You...you called me Abby?'

'Mmm.' He kissed her on the forehead. 'You seem to be breaking down all my defences. Next thing you know, I'll be telling you I love you.'

Abby froze in his arms. 'Don't say things like that!'

'Why not? You don't still hate me, do you, my love?' he asked, so tenderly that her own defences suddenly crumbled.

'You know I don't,' she choked out.

He sighed. 'I'm afraid I don't know any such thing. I don't really know anything about you. I certainly don't know your innermost feelings.'

'Are...are you saying you want to?' she asked tentatively, hardly daring to hope that she might really mean something to him.

'Yes. Yes, I do,' he said, sounding almost surprised at himself, yet quite pleased. 'And you can start by telling me about that nightmare.'

Abby wanted to. But she was still afraid.

'Don't be afraid,' he said gently, as though reading her mind. 'I'm not shockable.'

She breathed in deeply, then let it out in a shuddering sigh. 'You might be more shockable than you realise. But all right, Ethan, I'll tell you why I keep having this nightmare.'

'It's always the same one?'

'Always.'

'That sounds pretty traumatic,' he said thoughtfully. 'Want me to put on a light first? Or get you a drink?'

'No. Just hold me and listen.'

'My pleasure.'

'God, I don't know where to start.'

'Why not at the beginning?'

'The beginning?' she repeated.

Where on earth was the beginning?

For some strange reason, her mind flashed to that day when she'd come home from her Wednesday afternoon ballet lesson to find that her mother had left and wasn't coming back.

'She's run off with her current lover,' her father had bluntly told her, in that coldly aloof manner of his.

'But... but where's she gone?' she'd asked, dismayed and devastated. Her mother hadn't been much of a mother, but at only eleven she hadn't been quite sure of that yet. Though chronically self-obsessed, Stephany Richmond at least had a warmer and more engaging personality than her husband.

'I don't know and I don't care,' her father had returned coldly. 'She always was a slut. I only married her because she was pregnant with you. There hasn't been a decent-looking man visit this house she hasn't tried to seduce, and I dare say she succeeded more times than she failed.

'I see *you've* taken after her in looks,' he'd sneered. 'God knows what awaits me as a father in a couple of years. But be warned, Abigail. Shame me once with your behaviour and you'll be out on your ear without a penny. I won't be shamed by my daughter as well as my wife!'

And that had been that. Not a word of sympathy or comfort for the shocked and equally abandoned child, only abuse because she looked like her mother. The following day Abby had been sent off to boarding-school.

Now, why should that be the beginning? Abby puzzled.

Because, she finally realised, that had marked the start of her long, lonely, loveless teenage years which had produced the perfect victim for a man like Dillon.

She glanced up at Ethan in the darkness.

'You promise you won't misjudge me again? You promise you'll hear me out properly?'

'I promise.'

She sighed, and began at the beginning while Ethan listened.

She told him of her mother's defection and her dismissal to boarding-school, and of how her father's accusations and threats had made her fearful when boys had started being attracted to her. She had become reticent with the opposite sex and very wary, especially when she'd found herself having feelings she'd thought were a sure sign that she was a slut, like her mother.

So she spurned having a boyfriend to become a type of bluestocking, and in doing so found a certain satisfaction in her father's surprised praise. He gave her a year's trip overseas when she gained an excellent pass in her HSC—an elderly chaperon filling most of her time with visiting art galleries and museums and the great theatres of the world. Even so, men paid her attention, but once again she spurned them, despite feeling attracted to more than one.

On her return to Sydney, she began a science degree at university, and after two years' successful completion her father presented her with a red Mazda RX7 for her twentieth birthday, telling her it was because he was so pleased at how well she'd turned out.

Ironically, it was her car which first drew Dillon's attention. He came over to look at it in the uni car park, took a long second look at the pretty but naïve girl behind the wheel, then moved in for the kill.

Dillon.

A glamorous name for a very glamorous young man. Blond and bronzed and so beautiful, he took every girl at uni's breath away. And he wasn't just gorgeous to look at. He was intelligent and witty and charming as well, filling his days doing an endless engineering degree after failing several times. He even made his failing sound glamorous.

Abby didn't stand a chance once he directed his dazzling charm and personality full-blast upon her that day in the car park.

Yet she wasn't easy, sexually speaking. Heck, no. She'd built up quite a reserve against male overtures over the years. Dillon had to work damned hard to seduce her, gradually breaking down those quite unnatural barriers till she became the girl she'd probably been meant to be all along. Passionate and loving and sensual. Warm and affectionate and generous.

Once they became lovers, she really blossomed, physically speaking. She started dressing a little more sexily, leaving her shoulder-length hair down for a change, and generally being much more confident and comfortable with her female attractions. She even became a bit of a flirt, although her eyes were only ever for Dillon. He was her miracle-worker. She was mad about him.

When Dillon first asked her for small loans she simply gave him the money, telling him not to worry about repaying it. He always said he would but he never did, and soon he was spending more of her allowance, not to mention driving her car—his own being always in the smash repairs place. She often came home on public transport, which might have been a problem if her father had been around to notice, but he rarely was.

Abby kept on being putty in Dillon's hands for several months. Life had never seemed so wonderful. She was loved and needed and wanted.

Abby never realised that he was merely using her for the things a wild young man of his ilk couldn't get enough of or do without. Money. Sex. Decent wheels. Designer clothes.

And designer drugs.

God, but she was so naïve not to see that he was high on drugs a lot of the time. The way he drove. The way he could dance all night. The way he sometimes wasn't able to make love all that well.

Though perhaps that was due to his having already made love to someone else earlier on that day. She was later to discover that he had girls all over the place. She wasn't his only prey.

They were coming home from a dance party one Saturday night during her last year at uni when disaster struck. It was four in the morning and Dillon was speeding as usual. Abby tried to get him to slow down, but he merely laughed at her.

She looked down at her feet because she was afraid to watch the road and the oncoming traffic.

'I was still looking down when we ran a red light and smashed into another car,' she told Ethan. 'I hit my head on the dash and was knocked out cold. When I came to I was in the driving seat, my hands wrapped around the steering wheel. Dillon was nowhere to be seen. The woman driver in the other car was dead.'

Ethan switched on the bedside lamp and she glanced warily up at him. But he only looked shocked, not sceptical.

'When I was released from hospital after spending the night in with concussion,' she continued carefully, 'I was arrested.'

Ethan was frowning now. 'What was the charge?'

'Charges,' she corrected grimly. 'Culpable driving. Manslaughter and possession of narcotics. Dillon had kindly left his personal supply of cocaine tucked under the driver's seat,' she finished bitterly.

'Good God.'

'There were no other witnesses, you see,' she explained further. 'And it *was* my car. Dillon must have walked home. We weren't that far away from his parents' place. He told the police I'd dropped him off first. At that hour of the morning there weren't many people awake to corroborate or deny what he claimed.'

'What a bastard! Oh, you poor darling. I hope you had a good lawyer. Sounds like you needed one.'

She stared up at him. 'You...you believe me...'

'Well, of course I do. No one would make up a horror story like that! Besides, you're honest as the day is long. Even an old cynic like me can see that.'

Her eyes swam with tears, several spilling over.

'Hey!' he said softly, dashing them away with gentle fingers. 'What's all this about?' His fingers froze suddenly and he stared down at her. 'Hell, Abby, they found you guilty, didn't they? That bastard let you go to gaol for something he did.'

'Yes,' she choked out. 'I was sentenced to eight years. I...I got out in four. That was six months ago.'

'Oh, you poor darling. God, what a bastard. So what happened to *him*, do you know? I hope he died of an overdose, the creep.'

'No, I don't know what happened to Dillon and I don't really care any more.' And, strangely enough, she didn't.

'Don't care! Hell, he should be made to suffer for his crimes! I'd like to strangle him with my bare hands. Send the bastard straight to hell.'

'People like Dillon find their own hell on earth, Ethan.'

'You don't really believe that, do you?'

'Oh, yes. You take your Vanessa. She's not happy, you know. And as she gets older and loses her beauty she's going to be downright miserable. No one will love her or want her. You wait and see.'

'I've waited ten years and it hasn't happened yet,' he said drily. 'Anyway, I'd rather not talk about that witch, if you don't mind. Let's get back to you. You must have been absolutely devastated when you were first arrested.'

'Absolutely. My father refused to hire a decent lawyer for me. I had to settle for legal aid, but the lawyer assigned to me seemed to bitterly resent a millionaire's daughter using their services. Both the judge and jury appeared biased against me for the same reason. I was held up as an example of true justice—a spoilt rich bitch going to gaol for her selfish and amoral ways. Eight years was a pretty harsh sentence.'

'Oh, Abby... I'm so sorry... You make me feel terribly small. You've been through hell, whereas I—' He broke off suddenly, his dark brows drawing together in another puzzled frown.

'Now hold on, there! What about that story you told me about that rich older guy and his giving you all that jewellery and—?' He broke off again and glared at her, his expression becoming exasperated. 'That was your father, wasn't it? You played with words when you told me that, didn't you? Dillon was your only lover and your father paid for your trip overseas. Plus your pearls. Some sugar-daddy,' he scoffed. 'He was your *real* daddy!'

Abby gave him a sheepish look. 'Are ... are you angry with me?'

'I should be furious. Instead I'm merely flabbergasted. What a wicked little minx you can be sometimes, Miss Richmond!'

'Well, you had such an awful opinion of me, and I rather wanted you to go on thinking that way to keep you at bay. You see ... I wanted you to make love to me so badly. I was almost at screaming point for the wanting...'

'You wouldn't have kept me at bay forever, believe me,' he said thickly. 'I'd just about reached my own tether where my feelings for you were concerned.'

'We don't have to hide our feelings any longer, though, do we?' she murmured, placing her head on his bare chest and sighing a sigh of utter peace and contentment.

'Never.'

'I'm so happy you believed me, Ethan.'

'And I'm so happy you told me. Don't ever be afraid to tell me anything, my love.'

Abby's heart swelled with joy. He'd called her his love again, and this time she believed him. He did love her. He just wasn't ready to say it yet.

'And don't you be afraid to tell *me* anything,' she countered sleepily.

If she hadn't already been drifting off she might have felt the abrupt stilling in that stroking hand, might have worried when he made no reply.

CHAPTER FIFTEEN

THE golf-course was a picture—green and lush, with each fairway bordered by rows of those same pines that encircled the tennis courts. Clearly the drought hadn't affected this part of the countryside.

'Who's going to partner whom?' Henry asked as they assembled on the first tee.

'I'm easy,' Ethan said, and smiled at Abby.

She smiled back, her heart fairly bursting with happiness. It had been a marvellous day so far—had been since the first moment she woke that morning and remembered what had happened the night before. It was as though a great weight had been lifted from her shoulders in telling Ethan the truth, even better than when she'd told Miss Blanchford.

It had been equally marvellous to see how Ethan had ignored Vanessa's blatant overture towards him at breakfast, then at the barbecue lunch which had followed the morning's lectures. Ethan's ex had seemed most put out by his blunt rebuff on this last occasion, clearly stunned that he wanted nothing to do with her. She'd given Abby the most vicious look.

Abby had half expected the woman scorned to show up at the tennis courts that morning, where she and Ann had been having a re-match while the men were in conference, but there hadn't been a single sight of her. With a bit of luck she'd given up on Ethan and settled on seducing some other poor fool.

'If Abby plays golf like she plays tennis,' Ann warned, 'then I think we'll play the boys versus the girls.'

'She doesn't,' Ethan replied. 'Do you, darling?'

'Er...no. I'm a bit of a duffer.'

'Then she'd better play with you, Ethan,' Henry suggested.

'Fine by me,' he agreed happily. 'Don't look so worried, Abby. I don't mind if you can't play very well.'

Abby tensed inside. Gone was any idea of making Ethan look a fool by beating the pants off him. Now she had to concentrate on making him *not* look a fool by actually playing too well.

Hopefully, her rustiness would help her non-performance. She hadn't played golf in years. But she would still have to watch it. She'd been damned good once, her father having sent her to a sporting camp every summer for six years, where she'd been given professional lessons in all sorts of sports.

By adopting an appallingly crooked stance and a wayward elbow, Abby managed to hook her first drive out of bounds. Everyone commiserated on seeing her crestfallen face, then proceeded to show her what she should have done.

Ethan's ball sailed straight down the fairway for a couple of hundred yards and Henry's landed only a little shorter; even Ann's went a respectable distance, despite it scrubbing along the top of the ground.

'It's all in the swing-through,' Ethan explained patiently as they set off at a brisk pace to find her ball. 'I'll show you when we find your ball. *If* we find your ball,' he amended drily as they headed towards the pines. 'And you must keep your feet straight!' was his last piece of advice.

It wasn't her feet that she had trouble keeping straight for the eighteen holes, but her face. She hadn't realised how much fun it could be playing badly. Or having Ethan show her how to putt—his arms wrapped tightly around her, his body pressed against hers. Sometimes she genuinely played a bad shot, she was so distracted.

She almost made it round without raising Ethan's suspicions. The eighteenth hole was her undoing. It was a difficult par four, with a dog-leg corner to the right. A clump of tall trees made it very hazardous to cut the corner in an attempt to reach the green in one. Henry, by this time very smug at their imminent victory, suggested a bet on this last hole, placing a fifty-dollar wager on their combined scores.

When Ethan magnanimously agreed, Abby decided that his male pride had had enough to bear. So, when it came her turn, she lined up her ball and hit it with a great whack which sent it flying over the trees in a high arch—virtually the same shot Ethan had chosen earlier. Her ball landed right on the green, less than a metre from the hole and a couple of metres inside Ethan's ball. Both Henry and Ann had taken the conservative route— their balls down in the fairway at the corner, still a hundred metres from the green.

'Holy hell,' Henry said succinctly.

'Heavens!' Ann exclaimed.

'Did I do that?' Abby gasped, hoping she was using the right amount of astonishment in her voice. 'Your tips must be doing me some good, Ethan.'

Ethan remained suspiciously silent, though his suddenly narrowed eyes spoke volumes.

'Bit of a duffer, eh?' he muttered under his breath as they strode off the tee together, Ann and Henry going in a different direction. 'I hope you've had a good time, laughing at me behind my back.'

'Actually, I have,' she confessed impishly.

He shot her a savage look, which quickly dissolved into a helpless smile when she giggled. 'What on earth am I going to do with you?' he said, shaking his head.

'You could kiss me, if you like,' she said, puckering up.

'You're incorrigible.' But he did kiss her, with all the hunger and passion the Ethan of last Friday would never have displayed in private, let alone public. One kiss followed another, then another, his hands reaching down to curve over her buttocks and pull her into him as much as clothes would allow.

'You want to win this hole or don't you?' Henry shouted from the dog-leg corner after playing their shots.

'Coming!' Abby shouted back.

'Almost,' Ethan muttered blackly, and Abby burst out laughing. After a second so did Ethan, his face showing a startled delight at his own spontaneous humour.

He took his buggy with one hand and hers with the other. 'You know, Abby,' he said warmly as they walked companionably along, 'I could get used to this.'

I hope so, she thought. I sincerely hope so.

The evening was as successful and happy as the day, with cocktails followed by a formal five-course dinner. Abby's black crêpe sheath gown was as big a hit with Ethan as the coffee-coloured lace—her over-indulging herself at lunch and dinner resulting in another tight fit.

He seemed to like things tight on her, all night whispering erotic promises in her ear of what he was going to do to her later. And how often.

She laughed at his outrageous boasting at one stage, but he had the last laugh when he lived up to his promises, reducing her to a state of exhaustion.

'No more,' she said limply, some time after midnight.

'Chicken.'

'No—duck. A dead duck. So you can stop your cock-crowing. You win.'

'I didn't realise it was a competition.'

'You know it was. You were paying me back for this afternoon.'

'You know me well, Miss Richmond.'

'Too well, Dr Jekyll. Though I think it's back to Mr Hyde tonight.'

'What on earth are you talking about?'

She told him and he laughed. 'I always loved that story. And I always liked Mr Hyde better than Dr Jekyll. Which one do you prefer?'

'Not telling,' Abby said, yawning. 'Now, could we turn off the light and get some sleep? Henry tells me you have a riveting video of one of Dr Ballistrat's operations to watch tomorrow morning. You might need a few live brain cells if you're going to get anything out of it.'

'There's nothing Ballistrat can teach me that I'd want to know,' he scoffed. 'What are you and Ann doing tomorrow morning?'

'Ann's taking me into Bowral with her,' she mumbled into the pillow. 'She wants to visit the antique shops before we go back to Sydney after lunch.'

'Do you want any money to buy something?'

Abby knew that he was probably only being nice but she wished he hadn't offered. 'I don't want to buy anything.'

'You might want to stop off at one of those tea-houses, though, for morning tea.'

'I have enough of my own money for that.'

'Just asking. Don't get defensive.'

'I don't ever want you to think I want you for your money, because I don't!'

'I never thought that for a moment,' he returned drily. 'I know you only want me for my body.'

She rolled over, an exasperated glare in place, only to find him grinning down at her, dancing teasing lights in his beautiful blue eyes.

'Why, you!' she squealed, and began pummelling him in the chest and stomach.

He laughed and grasped her wrists, whipping her over onto her back and holding her arms up on the pillows above her head. When he secured both in one iron hold and began touching her again, she groaned her total exasperation. 'No, don't. I couldn't bear it again. I simply couldn't.'

She twisted beneath him, trying to get away from that merciless grip, that harassing hand and that marauding mouth. But his hold on her remained invincible, his ruthless attentions gradually achieving their aim.

'No, I told you,' she cried in fury and frustration, when it soon became obvious that it was her own feelings she was having to fight. 'No, no, no!'

'Yes, yes, yes, Abby,' he bit back, his lips and teeth momentarily stopping their torment of one of her nipples. 'Your body speaks far more truthfully and eloquently than your tongue. Shall I prove it to you?'

She was about to scream when he let her go, reaching over to switch off the light and leaving her to lie there, panting, for several long, agonising minutes, the dark and the quiet making her even more hotly aware of every throbbing, re-aroused nerve-ending she possessed.

And there seemed to be millions.

'So what's it to be, Abby?' he taunted at last from the black stillness of his side of the bed. *He* didn't seem to be breathing hard, or silently screaming with frustration. 'Sleep? Or me?'

'I see you've reverted to Mr Hyde again,' she bit out.

'Ah, but Mr Hyde does have his attractions for you, doesn't he?' And with a swift, savage movement, he pulled her over on top of him.

'Tell me you love me,' he rasped as he manoeuvred his steel hardness into her stunned body.

'You know I do,' she admitted on a raw whisper.

'Then say it!'

'I love you, God forgive me.'

'Then let God forgive the both of us, Abby,' he growled. 'For I love you too. More than I would ever have thought possible. No, don't say anything now, for pity's sake. Just keep doing what you're doing,' he urged, with his voice and his hands. 'This is how we found each other and this is all I want for tonight. We'll talk of the future on our way back to Sydney. *After* we've left this place well behind.'

'You're off in another world, Abby, aren't you?' Ann said, looking up from the table of knick-knacks she'd been browsing over. 'Making mental plans for your wedding?'

'In a way,' Abby confessed, still a little bewildered by Ethan's passionate declaration of love the night before. She couldn't help hoping that his plans included marriage, but something—some instinctive wariness, perhaps born of her bitter experience with Dillon—made her hesitate to hope too much.

She might have asked Ethan this morning to elaborate, except they'd slept in, then had to rush to get down to breakfast where the presence of Ann and Henry had rather precluded such a strange question. After all, they were supposed to be already engaged.

'And when is the wedding?' Ann persisted. 'Soon, I'll bet. If I know Ethan, he won't want to wait long after waiting all these years to find the right girl.'

'I'd marry him tomorrow, if I could,' Abby said with a quiet intensity.

'Oh, to be in love like that again!' Ann sighed expressively. 'It does wear off, though, that madness when you can't keep your hands off each other. Still, if you really love someone, that initial burst of uncontrollable lust gradually settles down to the most wonderful relationship, which includes the occasional burst of lust, a lot of contentment and companionship, and scads of security.

'There's nothing like that feeling of security—especially these days. The knowledge that you can trust your partner, both with your body and your life. Henry might look at other women, but I know he would never, ever touch one. He's my best friend, is my Henry. I will love that man till the day I die.'

'Oh, that's so beautiful,' Abby cried, tears flooding her eyes. 'That's what I want with Ethan, more than anything. That feeling of security. But I'm so afraid that he won't . . . that he might not . . .' She choked back a sob and dived into her handbag for a tissue.

Ann bustled her out of the antiques shop, murmuring apologies for having made her cry. 'You think Ethan might look at other women?' she asked when Abby had stopped weeping.

Abby shook her head. 'No. Not really . . .' If Vanessa had failed to turn his head this weekend, she couldn't see any other woman doing so easily. But the type of relationship Ann had just described seemed unattainable with Ethan. He'd said that he never trusted women. How could they be best friends without trust?

'You'll be all right,' Ann said, patting her hand. 'Trust me. I've seen a good few couples together in my life, and you two are the real McCoy. Let's forget the antiques and go have one of those Devonshire teas. There's a cute little tea-house just down the road. That's what you need—a cup of tea and a good dose of calories.'

Abby had to laugh. 'I think that's the last thing I need. Didn't you see me in that black dress last night?'

'Sure did. And so did all the men in the room,' Ann added drily. 'My Henry was most amorous last night, thanks to that dress of yours.'

Abby blinked her shock and Ann chuckled. 'You know, for a sophisticated-looking girl you have a way to go to learn about men and sex. Let me give you a piece of advice—never worry about a man looking. If he stops looking, then it's a good bet he's dead from the waist down and not much good to you anyway.'

'I...I'll keep that in mind.'

'Of course, that doesn't apply to a man-eater like Vanessa Ballistrat. If your man starts looking too closely at something like that, then you need to bring out the big guns.'

'The big guns?'

'Yeah, you either shoot her, or you get your man a hundred miles away. Quick smart.'

'Then it's as well we're going back to Sydney this afternoon,' Abby said thoughtfully.

'And none too soon, I'd say,' was Ann's final comment on the subject.

But it was already too late, Abby was to find out less than an hour later. Too late...

CHAPTER SIXTEEN

ANN dropped Abby off at the front of the hotel shortly after eleven. They hadn't spent nearly as long in Bowral as they'd intended, but that was all right by Abby. She still hadn't packed, and was anxious not to do anything to delay their departure after lunch.

'Thanks for the tea, Ann,' she said through the passenger window. 'See you at lunch.'

Ann drove off to park the car in the basement car park, Abby hurrying up the steps and into the hotel foyer. She moved quickly across the tiled floor and down the central hallway, and was approaching the door which led out to the back when it opened abruptly and an incoming person collided with her.

'Sorry,' she automatically apologised.

Vanessa seemed to take a moment to realise who she'd run into, while Abby could only stare at the woman.

There was no doubt that she was frighteningly beautiful, even in her present slightly flushed and flustered state. She looked decidedly dishevelled as well—her hair messy, her lipstick smudged, and the zipper on her black cat-suit open well past her bustline.

Abby was sure the creature was naked underneath the skin-tight outfit—her cleavage looked braless, her nipples starkly pointed, and not a pantie line showed anywhere. She looked as if she'd just had a hurried amorous rendezvous with someone. But not with her husband, obviously, since he was still at that moment delivering

174

his last lecture. Probably some poor fool she'd picked up down here.

A malicious smile began tugging at that sinfully sensuous mouth, a cold, cruel gleam entering those beautiful blue eyes.

'You're home early, sweetie.' She wagged a scarlet-tipped finger back and forth. 'Tut-tut. Never come home earlier than the boyfriend or hubby expects. It leads to trouble. After all, you told Ethan you'd be away all morning. But not to worry. It won't happen again. Not with me, anyway. I'm leaving shortly, and, frankly, I've outgrown men like Ethan. Still, the poor darling was desperate for one last sample of what he once couldn't live without, so I gave it to him. Wasn't that sweet of me?'

Abby tried not to believe the poisonous words. Tried with all her heart. Ethan loves me, she kept telling herself. He would not do this. She's lying.

But Vanessa's softly knowing laugh undermined her confidence. 'I wouldn't say anything to Ethan if you want to keep him, honey. I won't be back, after all. Phil and I are off on a world tour tomorrow. And so what if he thinks of me while he's doing it to you? What do you care? You'll be Mrs Ethan Grant. That's all you want, isn't it?'

Looking back, Abby would never know how she found the courage or the strength to do what she did. Somehow she dredged up a haughty yet at the same time pitying look, accompanied by a mocking laugh of her own.

'What a pathetic liar you are. Truly, you must think I don't know everything about you, you vile creature! My Ethan would never make love to you. He *despises* you. And you're quite wrong about my only wanting to be Mrs Ethan Grant. That's not it at all. I just want to be with him, to be his woman and the mother of his children.

'If you must know,' she added, out of some kind of desperate defiance, 'I'm already having his baby. Yes, that's right. I'm pregnant. Ethan truly loves me and I love him, and no scheming witch like you will ever break us up. So go round the world with your poor, pathetic husband. Keep screwing every man you fancy and keep screwing up your life. You'll end up a lonely old woman—a lonely, ugly woman whom no one will ever really want.

'Yes, go!' Abby raved on, finding some triumph as the blonde paled at her words. 'And be thankful that I'm letting you get away with your precious face and your precious boobs still intact. The only reason I am is that you're not worth going to gaol over. Heaven forbid!'

And, with another scornful laugh, she whirled and marched off, not once glancing behind, determined not to let that evil woman win in the smallest possible way.

But by the time she reached the door of her room Abby's courage was failing. Her head was whirling, her stomach churning, her heart pounding. What would she do if Ethan was inside...in this room...at this hour...when he should still be at the conference?

Abby's hand shook as she tried the door.

It was locked. Ethan wasn't inside after all. Vanessa *had* been lying!

She leant her head against the door and almost cried. How could she have ever let that woman make her doubt Ethan?

Sliding her key into the lock, she opened the door and walked in, a quick glance showing that the room was indeed empty. She had just closed the door behind her when the distinctive smell hit her nostrils.

It was Vanessa's perfume, the overpoweringly cloying perfume that she always wore. It permeated the whole room, its sickeningly sweet scent hanging in the air.

Abby clamped her hand over her mouth and slumped down on the side of the bed, gulping to stop herself from being sick. Closing her eyes, she tipped back onto the bed, only to be assailed by an even stronger whiff. She jerked upright as though stung, staring down at the quilt, knowing that Vanessa had lain there only recently.

She jumped to her feet and was staring despairingly down at the bed when the bathroom door was wrenched open and a naked Ethan just stood there. She stared, round-eyed at him, at the droplets of water still clinging to his body, at his appalled expression at finding her there.

'You weren't supposed to be back till twelve!'

Abby wanted to kill him. She wanted to kill them both. For clearly Vanessa hadn't lied. She'd lain here on this bed and Ethan had put his body into that vile woman's flesh.

Slowly, Abby became aware of a trembling deep inside, despite seemingly being in control. 'I'll be asking Ann and Henry if I can go home with them,' she said in a low, quavering voice. 'I don't want to ever see you again after this.'

'After what?'

If looks could have killed, he would have perished on the spot. 'Don't bother to lie,' she said coldly. 'I've just left Vanessa's charming company along the way. She told me what happened in here, but stupid me didn't believe her till I walked into this room. Now I know she *was* here. I can smell her. I can smell her on that bed. I can smell her everywhere. Is that why you had a shower, Ethan? To try to wash the smell of her off you?'

'I didn't touch her,' he denied fiercely. 'You have to believe me, Abby.'

When he took a step forward she put up her hands to ward him off. But she rather fancied it was the look on her face which did that. She could feel the bitterness burning in her eyes, the cold fury twisting her heart.

'I don't *have* to do any such thing,' she bit out. 'I won't be used and betrayed by a man a second time, Ethan Grant. I'll kill you first, do you hear me?' And, having said so, she felt her control break and she rushed at him—arms flailing, fists pounding, uncaring that she was the one sustaining the bruises as she struck out blindly and wildly. The pain in her heart was far greater than any pain in her body. He absorbed her blows for a while before stopping her, after which she sank down to the ground at his feet, sobbing hysterically.

'How could you?' she moaned when he sank to the floor next to her and gathered her up into his arms. 'How could you...?'

'I didn't, Abby,' he insisted brokenly. 'I swear to you. On my love for you, my honour as a doctor and my Hippocratic oath, I did not touch her. Do you think I could do such a thing after making love to you in that bed? Do you think I could ever go from your truly loving embrace to that slut's evil arms? God, Abby, I would rather die than be guilty of such treachery. I would rather die than have you lose faith in me and my love for you. Please, darling, say you believe me, say you still love me. I can't bear to think I might lose you. I just can't bear it.'

Abby heard the despair in his voice, saw the torment in his face, felt the trembling in his body.

He's telling the truth, she realised. He didn't touch Vanessa. He loves *me*.

All the pain drained away immediately, replaced by the deepest, sincerest regret. He'd believed *her* when she'd said she was innocent, whereas she hadn't believed him. 'Oh, Ethan...' She reached up and laid a gentle, apologetic hand against his grey, strained cheek. 'I'm so sorry for doubting you, even for a moment... Of course you wouldn't do a thing like that. Forgive me, my love. Forgive me.'

'Forgive you? I'm the one who should beg for forgiveness. I should never have let the bitch into the room, should never have given her the slightest opportunity to hurt you like that. I knew what she was like. How wicked and selfish she could be. But I wanted the chance to redress the mistaken opinion I might have given her the other night when I danced with her. I wanted the chance to tell her what I really thought of her.'

'What happened, Ethan?' Abby asked.

His shudder showed true revulsion. 'I still can't believe what she did. The woman is sick, I tell you. Sick.' He shook his head in disbelief.

'How did she get into the room with you? How did she know I wouldn't be here?'

'She must have overheard you and Ann at breakfast this morning, discussing your outing to Bowral, and planned her strategy accordingly. When we came out for morning tea from the conference, I was handed a written message from her. It said she needed to see me urgently—there was some crisis—and was waiting for me at the door of my room. I knew in my heart I should ignore the note, but I just couldn't. Curiosity, I guess, and that niggling need to have a type of revenge—even if it was only seeing the look on her face when I told her that I thought she was disgusting.

'She took my showing up as a sign I still wanted her, of course. Vanessa had snapped her fingers and stupid Ethan had come running. Once inside the room, she put on an act which would make your mind boggle. She tried tears at first—told me she still loved me, that she'd made a terrible mistake in marrying Ballistrat. She said he'd seduced her with the help of drugs, that he'd even made her into an addict for a while. She also said that he was a drunk and mistreated her, and that she wanted to leave him but was afraid.

'When that tack didn't seem to be working—I don't think I'd said a word at this stage—she turned to sex, as usual. I should have been expecting it, but I was still stunned when she pulled down the zipper of that disgusting outfit and stepped, totally naked, out of it. Perhaps she took my shock for a reluctant interest, for she started running her hands all over herself, reminding me that she used to do the same to seduce me when we were living together and I wanted to study but she wanted to make love.

'Which was true, I'm ashamed to admit. She knew all the tricks to turn on a man. She'd do anything, any time, anywhere to get what she wanted. What I didn't realise was that she'd do the same with any*one*. Back then, I was fascinated by her beauty, plus her total lack of sexual inhibition. What young man wouldn't be? This time, however, I felt nothing but revulsion. When she lay down on the bed and started touching herself more intimately, I actually bolted into the bathroom and started dry-retching into the basin.'

Abby could feel his disgust as he shuddered at the memory.

'When I came out,' he went on, 'she was gone. I dare say my actions spoke much louder than any words could have. Yet I felt no triumph, only a long, lingering revulsion and the feeling that I'd been made unclean by watching her, even for a moment. I locked the door, stripped off and had a shower. Even after I'd switched off the water I just stood there, unable to dry myself or function. Then I heard someone in this room. I thought maybe she'd hidden in the room somewhere, so I dashed out. Only to find you standing next to the bed, looking devastated.'

'I *was* devastated,' she admitted.

He held her close. 'God, I'd give anything to go back in time and just stay in that conference room. How could I have been so stupid? My only excuse is that I'd wanted some kind of revenge for so long, Abby. For what she did to me. She almost destroyed me all those years ago. I can't tell you...'

'But you can, Ethan. Tell me like I told you everything about Dillon. What else did she do to you, besides what you've already told me? I know there has to be something else... something awful.'

And he told her, in a hushed, hurt voice. How she'd been pregnant with their baby at the time of Philip Ballistrat's arrival at the hospital. She seemed thrilled, he said, almost as thrilled as he was.

Just that week, however, she'd found out that he wasn't as rich as she'd thought, that it would be years before he made that sort of money she wanted. He had watched her change before his eyes; watched her ruthlessly set out to seduce their famed visitor; watched his own future being slowly destroyed.

'Though she wasn't slow to destroy my baby,' he bit out. 'She got rid of that, quick smart.'

'Oh, Ethan, how horrible for you.'

'Seeing her again after all this time made me see it wasn't such a tragedy. Who would want *that* as the mother of his child?'

'It was still wicked.'

'She *is* wicked.'

'She didn't love you, Ethan. No woman who loved a man would do a thing like that. I would never get rid of your baby. Never!'

He hugged her to him. 'I know that.'

'I...I might even be pregnant now,' she confided to him. 'It's not all that likely, but it *is* possible. I'm notoriously irregular when my equilibrium is upset. And you've been upsetting my equilibrium for some time, Ethan.'

He held her away from him and stared down at her. 'Are you saying that when I offered you that morning-after pill the other day you might actually have conceived the night before?'

'Well, probably not...'

'But there *was* a risk?' he asked, frowning.

'Well, yes. You're...you're not mad with me, are you, Ethan? I mean, don't you want me to have your babies?'

His face was disbelieving. 'Don't I...?' His answer was to hug her again, so tightly that she could hardly breathe. 'Of course I want you to have my babies,' he said thickly. 'And I want you to be my wife. As soon as possible. Say yes, Abby. Please say yes. Make our engagement real.'

Abby shook her head in disbelief that he would think there was any other answer.

'You won't marry me,' he said bleakly. 'You don't trust me enough. And I don't blame you. I don't deserve you. I've been a pig. And a fool. God, I've been a fool for so damned long!'

She cupped his face firmly with her hands. 'Shut up, you silly man. Of course I'll marry you.'

'You will?'

'Yes, of course.' And then she laughed.

Ethan looked mildly affronted. 'This is a very serious moment, Abby.'

'I was just thinking of the expression on Sylvia's face when we tell her we're engaged. Not to mention Miss Blanchford.'

'Who's Miss Blanchford?'

'Don't worry. You'll know soon enough. By the way, how big is your house?'

'Too big.'

'Then you have a spare downstairs room for an old lady in a wheelchair?'

He smiled. 'Ah, so there really *is* an old lady with a wheelchair.'

Abby bristled. 'Did you ever doubt it?'

'Not really. Yes, of course we'd have a spare room downstairs.'

'That's wonderful!'

'I think I'm acquiring more than a wife here,' was his rueful remark.

Abby bit her bottom lip. 'She's like my family, Ethan,' she said pleadingly. She didn't add that her real family didn't want her any more, had never really wanted her.

'Well, why didn't you say so, darling?' was his wonderfully warm reply. 'Your family is my family, and my family is your family.'

'You don't think Sylvia will mind?' she asked hesitantly.

'Mind? She'll be delighted! She's been delighted with you all along. It was only her fool of a brother who couldn't see what a treasure she'd found for him. A treasure which I will guard and cherish all the days of my life.'

She snuggled into him and thought that it was she who had found the treasure. 'You're going to become my best friend, Ethan,' she said, remembering Ann's heart-wrenching words.

'I thought I was going to become your husband!'

'That too. And my lover. And the father of all my children.'

'Well, I'd better be or you're in big trouble. *How* many children did you say?'

'How many bedrooms does that house of yours have?'

'Oh, God, not that many!' he groaned.

'How many, Ethan?'

'Twelve.' His voice sounded very fragile.

'That many! Oh, I don't think I want that many children.'

'Thank God,' he muttered.

'I've only ever wanted ten.'

'Ten!' he squawked.

'Too many, still?'

'I think so.'

'How about eight?'

'Eight!'

'Six, and that's my final offer.'

'Six it is,' he sighed.

Abby snuggled into him again, feeling well satisfied. She'd only ever wanted six anyway.

'Ethan,' she said softly after a minute or two.

'Mmm.'

'What *did* you have in mind when you first came down here last Friday? I mean . . . you weren't ever really going to do anything bad, were you?'

'I won't lie to you, Abby. I wanted revenge. I wanted to make her suffer as she had made me suffer. I had a suspicion that she might make a play for me if I turned up. I'd heard the rumours about her husband's finances. I planned to lead her on for a while if she did, then crush her totally once she'd burnt her bridges behind her with Ballistrat.'

'But if that was your plan why did you hire me to come with you? Wouldn't you have been better by yourself?'

'Of course. But it seemed my feelings for you were already beginning to vie with my so-called feelings for Vanessa. I told myself you were the perfect salve for my male pride, plus a possible weapon to spur Vanessa on— since she always did enjoy ensnaring a man who belonged to someone else. Frankly, I told myself a whole lot of garbage just so I could be alone with you, Abby, my love.

'Once I found some excuses to kiss you, my need for revenge soon took a back seat. In fact, my intense hatred for Vanessa quickly watered down to nothing more than a cynical curiosity and a rather confused revulsion. That's why I danced with her. To ram home just how revolting I found her. My one regret is that I didn't tell her in so many words.'

'Don't worry, Ethan, I did it for you.'

'You what?'

Abby told him then—everything that she'd said to the woman.

'You didn't!' He sounded both astonished and admiring at the same time.

'I did, indeed.'

'Even the bit about her... um...'

'Boobs, Ethan. The word is boobs. I think I worried her slightly about that. She was certainly hugging her chest as she raced off,' Abby lied outrageously as Ethan's delight grew.

He laughed and hugged her tightly. 'Oh, that's priceless! I wish I'd been there to see it. There again, you *are* priceless, my darling.'

'Well, not quite, Ethan. I do have a price. Or I *did*. Which reminds me. I have a confession of my own to make about that.'

He looked alarmed.

'It's nothing terrible,' she soothed. 'But I don't think I agreed to come with you just because I needed that money. I think, underneath, it was because I wanted to go to bed with you.'

'Well, I certainly don't mind *that* confession.'

'But I don't think I loved you back then, Ethan. It was just sex to begin with.'

'It often is, my darling. That's the way of nature, and men and women. But it's not just sex now, is it, for either of us?'

'Oh, no,' she assured him. 'It certainly isn't.'

'I really, truly love you, Abby.'

'And I really, truly love *you*, Ethan. Only...'

'Only what?'

'Do you think you might put some clothes on? It's very distracting and disturbing.'

'I will, darling. I will... afterwards.'

DEBBIE MACOMBER

invites you to the

HEART OF TEXAS

Join Debbie Macomber as she brings you the lives and loves of the folks in the ranching community of Promise, Texas.

If you loved Midnight Sons—don't miss Heart of Texas! A brand-new six-book series from Debbie Macomber.

Available in February 1998 at your favorite retail store.

Heart of Texas by Debbie Macomber

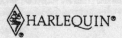

HARLEQUIN®

Take 2 bestselling love stories FREE

Plus get a FREE surprise gift!

Special Limited-Time Offer

Mail to Harlequin Reader Service®

3010 Walden Avenue
P.O. Box 1867
Buffalo, N.Y. 14240-1867

YES! Please send me 2 free Harlequin Presents® novels and my free surprise gift. Then send me 6 brand-new novels every month, which I will receive months before they appear in bookstores. Bill me at the low price of $3.12 each plus 25¢ delivery and applicable sales tax, if any*. That's the complete price, and a saving of over 10% off the cover prices—quite a bargain! I understand that accepting the books and gift places me under no obligation ever to buy any books. I can always return a shipment and cancel at any time. Even if I never buy another book from Harlequin, the 2 free books and the surprise gift are mine to keep forever.

106 HEN CH69

Name	(PLEASE PRINT)
Address	Apt. No.
City	State	Zip

This offer is limited to one order per household and not valid to present Harlequin Presents® subscribers. *Terms and prices are subject to change without notice. Sales tax applicable in N.Y.

UPRES-98

©1990 Harlequin Enterprises Limited

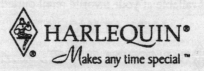

MEN at WORK

All work and no play?
Not these men!

July 1998
MACKENZIE'S LADY by Dallas Schulze
Undercover agent Mackenzie Donahue's
lazy smile and deep blue eyes were his best
weapons. But after rescuing—and kissing!—
damsel in distress Holly Reynolds, how could
he betray her by spying on her brother?

August 1998
MISS LIZ'S PASSION by Sherryl Woods
Todd Lewis could put up a building with ease,
but quailed at the sight of a classroom! Still,
Liz Gentry, his son's teacher, was no battle-ax,
and soon Todd started planning some
extracurricular activities of his own....

September 1998
A CLASSIC ENCOUNTER
by Emilie Richards
Doctor Chris Matthews was intelligent, sexy
and *very* good with his hands—which made
him all the more dangerous to single mom
Lizette St. Hilaire. So how long could she
resist Chris's special brand of TLC?

Available at your favorite retail outlet!

MEN AT WORK™

Coming Next Month

HARLEQUIN PRESENTS®

THE BEST HAS JUST GOTTEN BETTER!

#1971 THE RELUCTANT HUSBAND Lynne Graham
Unbeknown to Frankie, her marriage to Santino had never
been annulled—and now he was intending to claim the
wedding night they'd never had! But Santino hadn't
bargained on falling for Frankie all over again....

#1972 INHERITED: ONE NANNY Emma Darcy
(Nanny Wanted!)
When Beau Prescott heard he'd inherited a nanny with his
grandfather's estate, he imagined Margaret Stowe to be a
starchy spinster. But she turned out to be a beautiful young
woman. Just what situation had he inherited here?

#1973 MARRIAGE ON THE REBOUND Michelle Reid
Rafe Danvers had always acted as if he despised Shaan; he
even persuaded his stepbrother to jilt her on her wedding
day. Yet suddenly Rafe wanted to proclaim her to the world
as his wife—and Shaan wanted to know why....

#1974 TEMPORARY PARENTS Sara Wood
Laura had sworn never to see her ex-lover, Max, again. But
cocooned in a cliff-top cottage with him, watching him play
daddy to her small niece and nephew, it was all too easy to
pretend she and Max were together again....

#1975 MAN ABOUT THE HOUSE Alison Kelly
(Man Talk!)
Brett had decided women were unreliable, and right now he
wanted to be single. Or so he thought—until he agreed to
house-sit for his mother, and discovered another house-
sitter already in residence—the gorgeous Joanna!

#1976 TEMPTING LUCAS Catherine Spencer
Emily longed to tell Lucas about the consequences of their
one-night stand eleven years ago, and that she still loved
him. But she was determined that if they ever made love
again, it would be he who'd come to her....